DIARY OF A NEW YORK DOG

ISBN: 979-8-5177738-5-2
Printed in the United States
Illustrations by Alastair Bayardo
Layout and Design by Brett Davidson

www.diaryofanewyorkdog.com

DEDICATION

This book is dedicated to Elva Corrie, who urged me on through the years, the good times and the bad times, always ready for a good laugh.

TABLE OF CONTENTS

CHAPTER ONE
"Genesis"

I've been putting this off for several years now, but I have decided at last to finish my diary so that people will know what it's like being a dog in New York City. My good friend, Chandler, has agreed to put all my "bows" and "wows" and "arfs" and "woofs" into English so it will be readily understandable to everyone. At least to everyone who can read English. You may not be able to understand dog talk, but we dogs do. If you think dog talk is hard for you, can you imagine what it's like trying to understand a hip-hop lyric. Luckily, I got sent East instead of to California. I consider myself one of the lucky ones. At least sometimes.

1

First, I think I ought to tell you a little about me and my background. My name is Buster (more about that later). I was born in Kansas (spare me those "no place like home" jokes). Life wasn't pretty where I was born. There are a lot of nice-sounding names for my place of birth, but I prefer to call it a "puppy farm" because that's what they do-they breed puppies, pluck them away from their mothers, fathers, brothers and sisters when they're about five weeks old and ship them all over the country. I ought to know because that's what happened to me.

I am a miniature schnauzer. We're of Swiss and German descent. My ancestors were great hunters in the Black Forest and other such exotic places. But we were much bigger then, and there are still a few of us who are referred to as "standard" schnauzers. But most of us have been bred down to what is known as "miniature" schnauzers. I even understand that some breeders are trying to make us even smaller into "toy" schnauzers. And let's not forget the giant schnauzers. Before you know it, you'll be able to wear one of us around your neck on a chain. It's what I call de-evolution, or back to the amoeba.

I'll never forget the train ride from Kansas to New York City. We were all huddled together in this dark compartment, and all we could hear was clickety-clack, clickety-clack all night and all day. Even now, when the sun begins to go down and it starts getting dark, I still hear that sound, and I'm afraid.

Life in the pet shop was interesting but not fun. I met a lot of other dogs from all over, but the owners would never let us socialize

2

together. That didn't stop us from talking to each other. There were two other schnauzers in the shop, except I was the only one from my birthplace to be sent there.

About the third day I was there, another schnauzer and I were put into the front window of the store. We could look out and see tall buildings and lots of people walking by. I joked to myself that this sure wasn't Kansas anymore. People would press their noses against the glass and a lot of them would purse their lips together as if they were trying to kiss us. And there was one horrid little girl who stuck out her tongue at me, but I turned my back on her and went to sleep.

That day it suddenly dawned on me what I was doing there when a man and a woman came into the store and picked my companion up, petted him, held him to their faces and handed him over to the owner. The next thing I saw was that my friend had been put into a cardboard carrying box and was being taken away by those two people. Sold! Into slavery? I was panicked. I started running around in the window, not sure of what I was doing. Finally, the owner came and put me back in my cage. At least I was safe for another day.

A lot of people looked at me for the next couple of days, and several of them asked the owner to open my cage and let them hold me. At first I was afraid, but then I realized that they weren't going to hurt me so I just relaxed and tried to enjoy it. But I didn't feel that I wanted to be bought by any of them. Not until Andy came to the store.

It was my day to be in the front window, and there was a new little female schnauzer who had just arrived who was there with me. She didn't have a clue as to what was going on, and I really didn't want to tell her too much since I was afraid she might get really frightened by it all. Also, I think she was still a bit shell-shocked from her train ride into town.

Anyway, this really nice-looking guy, about thirty, stopped in front of the window and looked in. He had the kindest eyes I had ever seen, and I suddenly realized that more than anything in the world, I wanted to be bought by him. I really went all out. I jumped and wagged what was left of my tail. I tried to roll over, but I made a mess out of that. But something did the trick because he came into the store and asked the owner to let him hold me.

I pretended I was thirsty just so I could go over to the water and get my nose wet. Some instinct told me Andy would like me better if I had a wet nose. When he picked me up, I pushed my nose up against his cheek and started licking him. What a performance! I could see he was beginning to melt so I just kept licking as hard as I could until finally he handed me to the owner and told him he wanted to buy me. It had worked!

I was placed in a box with a soft cloth on the bottom, and then the box was closed. Darkness again! Andy carried the box out of the store and started walking to his apartment. I tried to see through the holes they had left for air to circulate, but I couldn't see a thing. However, I could hear all sorts of sounds: people walking and talking; cars going by; buses; a loud siren at which I started to howl because it hurt my ears. But then Andy opened a door, I heard another door slide open and we started going up in what I later found was an elevator. The door slid open again, and we left the elevator. Andy

4

walked a little way and then unlocked another door.

He reached down and opened the box up and set me down on the floor of his living room. I was so excited that I had a new home that I couldn't help myself and wet all over the floor.

Andy got this stern look on his face and gently hit my behind. "No, no, no!" That's when I realized my bodily functions were going to have to be disciplined, and I felt I could do it, even though it might take a little time.

Andy picked me up and took me through the apartment. It wasn't very big but there was lots of sunlight and it was mine! I was so happy that I reached up and licked Andy's ear. And then he kissed me on top of my head. I was in love.

CHAPTER TWO
"What's in a Name?"

I started to settle into my new home when all at once I came to a startling realization. I didn't have a name! Andy never gave it to me. Surely he wasn't going to just call me "hey you" or something like that.

I shouldn't have worried. That first night four of his friends came over to meet his new arrival, me. They were very nice and petted me and talked baby-talk to me, and I felt like the king of the world.

Then one of them asked Andy what my name was. He said he didn't know but suggested that maybe they ought to pick a name that night. My mother's name was Lady Windermere and my father's name was Duke of Wellington so I was sure Andy and his friends would see that I was from good stock and would name me appropriately. Besides, they had my pedigree which showed my parents' names and the fact that there were champions all through my blood line. You can look it up.

Andy's friend, Paula, suggested "Spot". I was sure she must be joking. But she said, "As in 'see Spot run'. You know, the old Dick and Jane books we had in first grade."

Well, I was furious and decided that no matter who tried to call me "Spot", I wasn't going to pay any attention to them. Sure enough Paula tried to pick me up, calling me "Spot". I wasn't having any part of that and ran to the other side of the room. She kept saying "Come here, Spot" but I pretended I was waiting for a bus and couldn't hear a word she said. She finally shut up.

Andy looked at me. "I guess he doesn't like the name."

Paula answered, "That's ridiculous. How could he know one name from another or have any feelings about it?"

That was really hitting below the belt. I thought very seriously about going over and biting her ankle, but I realized that violence would do me no good. I had to be cool.

Bill suggested, "Call him Fido, spelled P-H-I-D-E-A-U-X, the French way."

A poodle's name! Never. Thank goodness Andy didn't like it saying I wasn't a Fido type. How right he was. I thought I saw my pedigree on the floor by the sofa so I rushed over to the paper, put it in my mouth and went over to Andy. Surely he would get the message!

Paula said, "Isn't that cute? He fetches."

I tried very hard to barf all over her, but I just couldn't manage it. How insensitive can one person be? Andy took the paper, looked at it and then looked at me. "You're trying to tell me something, aren't you?"

I wagged my tail and let my pink tongue hang out a bit. That ought to get him.

Paula again. "What could he possibly be telling us, Andy? Dogs can't read." I vowed to myself that someday she was going to get it.

"Well, we were talking about a name for him, and he brought his pedigree over to me. Don't you think there is some coincidence in that?"

"Not at all." Paula was still a jerk.

"But let's suppose he is trying to say something," Kate said. "What could it be?"

Bill answered, "Maybe he wants to be named one of the names of his ancestors."

Before Paula could utter one of her inanities, I ran over to her trying to decide whether to pee on her shoe or bite her ankle. I chose the ankle. But just a warning nip.

Paula screamed, "He bit me!"

Andy came over to me and scolded me while hitting my backside. But he didn't hit too hard even though I put on a good act for Paula; I acted as if I had been mortally wounded. I think Andy knew that Paula was out of line with me. At least I hope he did.

Kate picked up on this whole scene. "I think your puppy really does want a name from his ancestors." Good for her!

But Bill, Henry and Andy didn't get it, especially Henry. "You don't know what you're talking about, Kate. He should have a plain old dog name."

Kate shot back at him. "Why don't you just call him Buster, then?"

I put my head on the floor, chin down, and covered my face with my paws. I tried not to listen anymore. I had this sinking feeling that my fate had been sealed.

Andy laughed. "Yes, Buster is a great name for him. A real name; nothing pretentious. That's perfect."

Kate said, "I didn't mean for you to actually choose the name Buster; I was just being facetious."

"Too late now," Bill said. "It's Buster!"

I gave a little whimper and rolled over onto my side, resigned to my fate. Andy saw it and took pity. "His name is 'Buster'."

Andy broke out a bottle of champagne. Of course I wasn't offered any. Well, I was only eight weeks old, but still he could have been polite. He and all his friends toasted me with the bubbly and inside I smiled.

CHAPTER THREE
"Basic Training"

The bubble of my new euphoria at having a home was about to burst. The reason -training! Now, don't get the wrong impression that I'm stubborn or anything like that, but I like to do things at my own pace, in my own way, and in my own time. But Andy was very impatient.

We began with toilet training. What a laugh! Easy for him to tell me to go squat on some smelly newspaper, getting the ink from the type all over my little paws. He had his own separate room to do his business in while I was left in full view of whoever was visiting. I

11

didn't like this one little bit so I resisted whenever possible.

Sometimes I would sneak into his bathroom and use the bathmat. At least no one could see me there. And besides, isn't that what bathrooms are for? But Andy was always very upset whenever I did this. After a few spankings, I decided to give up and use the newspapers.

What I resented even more was what Andy called "tricks". "Roll over". "Sit". "Beg" (beg?). "Paw". Ad infinitum. What did he think I was going to be anyway, a trained seal? A circus animal? I thought we'd just be friends, not that I had to perform for him whenever he felt like entertaining friends. What was in it for me? Yes, I know, I'd get a little, and I mean little, treat after I would perform, but it wasn't worth it.

I did try, but my heart wasn't in it. I decided that I would perform "sit" and "paw", which could be executed from the "sit" position, where I would lift my left paw for him to shake. He used to joke that I was a southpaw (some baseball expression, I'm told). But I wasn't going to be caught dead rolling over, playing dead or begging. That was for stupid dogs, and I was anything but that.

That's when I realized I was really going to have to train Andy, not the reverse. He was smart. Soon he'd understand that schnauzers (at least this one in particular) were only going to do the tricks we wanted. And I was right. After a couple of weeks, he gave up. I heard him tell his friends later that I could only do two "tricks". Hah! I could do all of them in a heartbeat; I just didn't want to.

Eventually, I grew old enough to be taken for what Andy

called "walks" and what I called being dragged around the block. I like to sniff all the smells and feel the excitement of being on the sidewalks of New York. But Andy never seemed to have time for a proper walk. It made me very sad although I admit I did linger at certain spots just to see how long his patience with me would last.

All things considered, I think I've been very good about my training. I know I could have obeyed a lot sooner, but if I had done that, it wouldn't have been nearly as much fun. I loved seeing him turn up his nose and turn his face away when he picked up all those soiled newspapers. If he thought it was so awful, what about my feelings. I smelled the same stuff he did, but I had to sit in it. Ugh! Someday people will learn that pets are people too. I'm not a dog; I 'm a small gray person!

CHAPTER FOUR
"Toys R Not Me"

Andy went wild at the pet store. He didn't take me with him or maybe he wouldn't have done what he did. He came home with a sack full of things which he pulled out one at a time in front of me.

"Look at this mouse, Buster. Do you like it?" Then he threw it across the room. "Go get it!" I looked up at him as if he were crazy but luckily he couldn't decipher my expression. As I saw it, I had two choices only: go to the mouse or stay where I was. Dilemma time. I thought to myself, "I'll do it this once and maybe that will satisfy him."

So I went over to the other side of the room and picked up the mouse. It squeaked the minute I put it in my mouth. I jumped back; I hadn't counted on that. How disgusting! And it tasted like cheap

15

rubber, not that I knew what expensive rubber tasted like. But it had to be nicer than this. I left the mouse alone and came back to Andy's side.

"Didn't like the noise, huh?" Andy asked.

I didn't say anything since I don't speak English.

"Maybe this will be better." He went into the bag and pulled out a metal thing that looked like a cat. It was a wind-up toy which he proceeded to wind up and place on the floor in front of me. It started toward me, and I stepped back a couple of steps not really knowing what to expect. But it kept coming straight toward me.

Andy was laughing at me now thinking I was scared of this thing. I had no choice. I took my paw and slapped the cat across the room where it lay on its side unwinding making the most awful noise.

"I struck out again, I guess." Andy seemed resigned. "But I know what you can't resist."

Out came a rawhide bone that was almost as big as I was. It smelled good (I guess that was the formaldehyde) and I tried to bite into it. There wasn't any place I could get a grip though so that each time I would try to bite the bone would roll further across the room. Then it came to me what to do; I jumped on top of it and held it under me. At least it didn't move, but of course, I couldn't chew it either. Andy came over to me and took the bone. I, of course, made a low growl as if I didn't want him to touch my property, but that didn't stop him. Maybe he knew I didn't really mean it.

"We'll have to save that for when you get bigger. I should have gotten you a smaller one." I would have been happy with some nice chewy dog biscuits, but I didn't want to hurt his feelings. He really was trying; it's just that he didn't know how to buy for me. But then how could he since he'd never had a dog before.

Next came a stuffed moose which was just about the same size as I was. He put it down next to me, and to show him what a primitive, wild, ferocious animal I was, I grabbed its neck in my teeth and shook it as hard as I could. He really liked that! His eyes lit up and he started saying, "Kill, kill, kill." The more he talked the more furious I became with the moose until all of a sudden the stuffing inside the moose started to burst out of the animal. I started to choke on all that cotton or sawdust or whatever it was so I threw the moose down and backed away from it.

Andy seemed sad. "The poor moose," he crooned. "You killed the moose." He pretended to cry. All of this from the man who had been yelling "kill, kill" at me. Sometimes you just can't figure people out.

Then he pulled out something that looked like a cheeseburger but it was made of rubber. Give me a break! He couldn't really think I wouldn't know the difference. These toy manufacturers must make these toys for people, not for dogs.

You can't fool us that easily.

He saved the best for last, and I was really excited when he pulled a red rubber ball out of the bag. He rolled it across the floor toward me, and I grabbed it between my paws and nestled myself over it. He came over to try to take it away from me, but it was small enough that I could put in my mouth and run, which is what I did. I

17

got under the couch and scrunched myself against the wall holding the ball away from him.

But he was bigger and stronger than I was, and I didn't want to bite the hand that feeds me so I let him think he'd won. I pretended not to care what he did with the ball. I concentrated on my dinner bowl until he finally gave in and threw the ball to me. I swatted it with my paw and then chased after it. This was fun! And Andy seemed really pleased that I had at least taken to one of the toys.

I realized that I was being a real ingrate to Andy. Here he had gone and spent all this money to make me happy and I was acting like a prima donna (or a primus donnus I guess is the masculine). I really began to feel guilty. I know, you don't think a dog can feel guilty, but I'm here to tell you he can.

I went around the room and picked up each toy, one by one, and brought them back to Andy and put them into a neat little pile, looked up with the most affectionate eyes I could muster and wagged my tail. That did it; Andy picked me up and hugged me as I licked his ear, which got me a dog biscuit, and isn't that what it's all about?

CHAPTER FIVE
"The Real Poop"

I really thought Andy had gone crazy or maybe had just gotten weird or something. Or maybe he had some strange fetish that was just beginning to manifest itself.

When I was very young, I didn't pay much attention to it. But now that I was older I began to notice it in a big way and couldn't make the least bit of sense out of it.

Every time I pooped when we went for our walk outside, Andy was picking it up! Sometimes, he'd just throw.it away in a garbage basket on the street; sometimes, he'd stuff it into one of those plastic bags you get at the supermarket and carry it back to the apartment.

19

But there was no doubt about it - he was obsessed with my poop!

Now this is very unnerving. First of all I had to endure the humiliation of having to poop on the street in front of whoever might be passing by. That was bad enough. But now this! What would people think? It got so that every time I pooped I tried to pretend I wasn't with Andy or I'd start immediately to walk quickly down the street with him bending down behind me scooping my leftovers into a paper towel or sometimes a piece of newspaper. I was at my wit's end, and I knew I had to think of a plan to stop this. The idea came to me on one of my walks. I spied a big, round metal circle near the corner. It was the cover for the water mains or something like that. And it had one or two round holes in it.

This was my salvation! The holes were just big enough. With a soaring heart I immediately went onto the metal circle, squatted directly over one of the holes and pooped. Bingo! Robin Hood's arrow couldn't be more accurate.

I turned and looked at Andy. He was just standing there holding a paper towel with this look of frustration on his face. For a minute I thought he was going to cry which made me feel really bad. Why had I done such a thing? It didn't cost me anything to let him have my poop. I wasn't ever going to use it again. And if it gave him pleasure, there really wasn't any harm in it.

Andy's look turned instantly from crying to laughter. He started to giggle at first and then he really let it come out. All this because I had pooped into the manhole, as I learned it was called.

He leaned over and patted me on top of the head. "You are the smartest dog in the free world."

Well, of course I knew I was and it was nice of Andy to acknowledge it. But what hidden meaning did all of this have? A man walking by commented, "That's a clever way to keep the New York City streets clean."

From then on I have always tried to find a manhole cover during my walks. I have to confess there are times when I miss the hole, put I am always confident that Andy will be right there with his paper to scoop the poop for his own pleasure.

It's funny that Andy will very often tell his friends who are over for drinks or a visit about my relationship with the manhole covers, and all his friends laugh like crazy.

I wonder if they would laugh if I told them about his weird poop fixation. But of course I never will. Until now, that is.

22

CHAPTER SIX
"Sunday in the Park"

One of my first joys when I was old enough to do it was to go to the park. We lived near Beekman Place on East 50th Street so the park we went to first was the one at the bottom of the hill from Beekman. All those stairs! It wasn't too bad going down but coming back up was murder. I made what I believe to be a very astute observation at the park. When dogs are on leashes, they tend to be much more aggressive toward other dogs. But when we're off the leash and allowed to run around, sniff and pee without supervision, we're not such a bad lot. Of course, there are always exceptions which

I found out a few times, but by and large "we are marvelous creatures" as Professor Higgins would say.

The Beekman Place "park" was really just a concrete area almost devoid of grass or plants. Very urban. And even though I met a lot of dogs, many of them " in society" as they were quick to tell me, I longed for something more. Dirt! To dig in shrubbery! To lift my leg on. Frankly, I was tired of car tires and garbage cans. A dog can do that just so long before the old primal urge for more takes hold.

So it was with a happy heart and wild expectation that I approached my first visit to Central Park. I had heard rumors from some of the dogs at Beekman Park that this was it. Nirvana! Dog heaven! I only hoped they hadn't been joshing me or getting my hopes too high. When we got out of the cab (I wasn't about to walk the two miles or so to the park), I saw it - paradise in Manhattan.

Great stretches of green lawn and trees and even a lake. Of course, these paws of mine never touched water, and I certainly wasn't about to change that now. We terriers don't like water which Andy found out the first time it rained and I put on brakes at the front door. I have a very strong neck and try as he might, I was going to win the battle to show him once and for all that I am not waterproof.

But I digress. Don't get me wrong about Central Park. It wasn't a great expanse of lawn without people. There were tons of people - people walking, people running, people walking their dogs, people lying on blankets without all their clothes on (I don't mean naked).

Andy took me to the place where he claimed many of the dogs

24

played. I wanted so badly to be off the leash. Andy met this girl who was walking a poodle, and when she asked if I was allowed off the leash, Andy told her I wasn't trained yet so he had to be careful. Not trained? I could have done everything he asked me, but of course I didn't want to tip my hand too soon. Think of all the treats (dog biscuits) I would never eat if I had responded too well at first. But, of course, all things come with a price, and I was paying it because of my passion for biscuits.

The other part of the price was that Andy kept me on the leash. I still met a lot of other dogs, and most of the time everything was very friendly until this completely supercilious Afghan hound came up and started to make trouble by calling me declassé. That refugee from a Chinese opium den had a lot of nerve and I let him know it. But Andy and his owner resolved the dispute by pulling us apart. If Andy had only known what he said and the way he said it, I really think he would have let me finish that mutt off. I'm sorry to use the "m-word", but that's the only way to describe him.

I was on one of those twenty-five foot expandable leashes which left me a lot of room to run. Even though I wasn't really a jogger, I had heard it was good for the heart so I jogged and I jogged. Besides, I thought it would be good for Andy to have a workout.

When I had finally exhausted him, we went to the outdoor cafe where they let dogs come (no discrimination!) He had a ham and Swiss on rye and a small bag of potato chips. What did I get? A paper cup filled with water. Now I ask you, is that fair? And that expression "a dog's life" is supposed to mean "easy". Hah!

The girl we met, her name was Betsy, was sitting at the cafe by herself, with her poodle too, of course. I saw Andy eyeing her, and I think she noticed it, too. She smiled, and when she did that, I knew Andy was going to make a move. It's such a burden always being right. Before I knew what was happening, I was being dragged over to her table. Hey, what about my water? I'm not going to share with that poodle. But Andy was in another world now so poor Buster (ugh, that name) was forgotten.

After enduring about ten minutes of this, I finally put my paws up on Andy's leg and began panting, hoping he'd get the picture. He didn't; but Betsy looked over at me with this very tender expression and said, "I think Buster wants some water."

The light bulb finally clicked on over Andy's head. "I forgot that I left his water at the other table." He reached down and patted me on the head. "I 'm sorry, Buster. Do you forgive me?" What was I to do? So I licked his hand and tried to put a forgiving expression on my face, and I guess that cleared it all up. Andy was happy; Betsy was happy; and I got a cup of water.

We hung around the cafe for another half hour or so which was pretty boring. The poodle was only interested in her nails and her coiffure which couldn't have interested me less. Some of those French dogs can be so tiresome. All that meant was that I lay by Andy's feet and pretended to sleep. But what I really wanted was to get back to the apartment and maybe get a dog biscuit for my troubles. All in all, though, Central Park is wonderful.

CHAPTER SEVEN
"Noel and I Don't Mean Coward"

This diary I know isn't in any logical order, but I feel like talking about Christmas right now so you'll have to bear with me. I have to confess it's my favorite time of year, at least indoors. I always know when it's Christmas because Andy comes home carrying a big tree all tied in rope. It's always an evergreen tree, usually a spruce. I'm glad he likes spruce trees because I like them too.

He sets the tree up in the same corner every year, I guess because it's near a window where neighbors can see the lights and know that Andy is celebrating Christmas, too. When I get up on a chair and look out of the window, I see other apartment windows with trees and lights and ornaments. It makes Christmas a very festive time.

I don't know why it is but every year Andy seems to have trouble getting his tree to stand up straight. It always seems to want to fall over or at least tilt, and every year he ends up tying ropes from the tree to the wall to keep the tree from falling. But it doesn't seem to bother him, and of course, it doesn't bother me either.

From the top shelf in his closet Andy brings down his "Christmas box" full of lights and ornaments and other good things like stockings that will be stuffed with good things on Christmas morning. I've already caught on to that. I also know he's the one who puts the goodies in the stockings, not Santa Claus. But I never let on that I've seen him doing it when he thinks I 'm asleep. You have to be pretty smart to fool me.

I always loved the Christmas box because it had so many beautiful things in it. Andy had a lot of ornaments. I think he got compulsive every year at Bloomingdale's Christmas store because a lot of his things came from there. I would sit and watch him carefully arranging the balls and trumpets and angels and other things onto the tree branches, just like an artist making a sculpture. One time one of the ornaments fell, and I ran over and picked it up in my teeth by grabbing onto the little round metal piece at the top. I brought it over to Andy and dropped it in front of him. Andy was delighted. "What a good boy! " he said. And then he gave me a pat on the head. No biscuit to be seen. It was then I decided that if I went to the trouble of fetching his stray ornament and the only reward was a pat on the head that there was no future in that for me. So I just sat and watched. Andy had already put the lights onto the tree first, and when he finished with the ornaments, it was time to put the silver icicles on. He had several boxes of them, and Andy loved to load the tree down with icicles. Of course, they got all over the floor at the same time as they got all over the tree. But they really made the tree sparkle, especially when Andy turned the tree lights on and the apartment lights off.

I was hoping he would have eggnog again to celebrate Christmas because I really liked it. He never knew I took a few sips out of his glass last Christmas when he wasn't looking. I was very patient and waited for my chance. When he went into the bathroom, I raced over to his glass, and EUREKA! There was still some left so that I would be able to taste it and not leave any evidence that any of it was gone.

Just as my little pink tongue was having its taste buds titillated to the max, I looked up and there he was! Caught red-handed or eggnog-mouthed as it actually was. Andy was staring at me harshly. I did my equivalent of a dog shrugging his shoulders and tried to look as innocent as possible. I mean, after all it's Christmas! Can't I get a little Christian charity at this sacred time of year? It must have worked because he started to smile and offered me another few licks.

I confess to two Christmas sins (I don't include the eggnog episode as a sin since I don't think it is). One, I love to bat the Christmas tree ornaments with my paw. Two, I eat the icicles. As far as the first one goes, if I'm very careful, the ornaments merely sway when I tap them, but if I'm too rough, they fall off. I don't think Andy is aware that I'm the reason he comes in some mornings and finds a couple of ornaments on the floor.

But he knows for sure about the icicles. You see, they aren't digestible so when he sees my poop glitter in the sunlight from the pieces of ice cycle, there isn't much I can do to defend myself. If only I had Johnnie Cochran to play the dog card for me! But Andy doesn't really seem too upset about the icicles. I mean, he's got a lot more on the tree than he ever needed in the first place.

Christmas morning! The stockings come down and it's dog biscuit heaven. Andy lets me have extra biscuits on Christmas morning. I always think I'm going to pretend to eat a couple of them but really hide them away for later, but somehow when they're there in front of me, I have no will power and just gobble them up.

Andy doesn't get me those rawhide bones anymore because I really just don't like them. But he always finds one or two new toys for me to play with. I think he buys them more for himself than for me because he knows I'm not really a toy person. Actually, I'm not a person but as I've said before, anyone who knows me thinks of me as a small gray person.

The highlight of Christmas morning is unwrapping the presents. Andy lets me help. Sometimes I try to use my paws but mostly it's my nose. I just dig in under the wrapping paper and lift, lift, lift. I use my nose the same way I do when I dig, first the paws to loosen the dirt and then the nose to shove it toward one side. It works on wrapping paper too but not as well. And the crinkly-crunchy sounds are so much fun!

It's all over so fast, but at least we have the tree for two or three weeks, and that makes a happy memory till next year.

CHAPTER EIGHT
"All Alone by the Telephone"

I might as well get this off my chest right now - I hate being left alone in an apartment all day. It's really boring, or at least it was until I found a solution which I'll tell you about later.

The first time it happened, of course, I was very young and slept a lot anyway so I didn't even think about it. It was routine. On Mondays through Fridays Andy went to work and Buster got left alone. But as I grew older, I started minding it a lot.

At first I thought I would just sleep till he got back. But I couldn't sleep that long and then be expected to sleep all night, too. I think you have to be bitten by a tsetse fly to be able to do that. And I don't believe there are a lot of tsetse flies in New York City. So sleep wasn't the solution.

I never learned to play cards so solitaire wasn't an option; my paws just weren't made for gripping a pencil or pen or for using a computer so I couldn't write. If I had been able to do that, Chandler would have been out of a job writing all this down for me.

I could just lie there and think, but what was I going to think about? Chasing cats? Dreaming of a humongous soup bone that was mine, all mine? Deciding whom to vote for for president? It didn't make a lot of sense.

Someone once said, "all good things come to those who wait" and it must be true because after waiting all that time in a complete state of boredom, it happened.

When Andy left for work that fateful morning, he accidentally left the television on. Since there was nothing else to do, I went in and sat in front of it to see what fascinated him so. It was wonderful!

I've heard the rumor that dogs don't see in color and don't know what's happening on the television set. Let me put the record straight. We can and we do; I'm the living proof.

I watched all kinds of shows from talk shows to game shows and then came the soap operas. They were my favorites. All that angst; all that drama; all that incest and cheating and back-biting. If real life was like that, I was glad I was a dog. People have unbelievable problems!

Then a magical thing happened. There was a clicker that I saw

34

Andy use, and when he did, the picture on the television changed. Magic! Andy had left the clicker on the sofa where I was sitting. I went over to it and tried to pick it up the way Andy did. But of course I couldn't. But in trying to do it, I accidentally hit a button on the clicker, and the picture changed. It was a totally different soap opera. Of course, the people were doing pretty much the same things as they were in the other soap opera.

I watched that one for about fifteen minutes. Then I thought I would try the clicker again to see if I could make the picture change again. I wasn't sure which button to hit so I just guessed. The sound got louder, but the picture didn't change. Wrong choice.

I tried again and the sound got softer. Wrong again. But on my third try I hit a different button and the picture changed again. It was a show about bugs! Ugh! Why would anyone watch that? People are really weird.

I quickly changed the picture again and got another soap opera. This one was really good. There was a murder trial going on. At least this was a little different from the other two. But then it got back into the sex and the nastiness which was getting boring, but I was addicted and I knew it.

The next day Andy turned the set off after watching the "CBS Morning Show". I didn't know how to make the television set go on. It was very frustrating. I found the clicker on the sofa and started to bounce on it up and down frantically hitting every button that I could. The set went on! I had no idea how I had done it, but there it was, and I settled in for a day of TV. But what would Andy think if the set was

35

still on when he got home. He knew he had turned it off because I heard him muttering to himself about wasting electricity or something like that. And then it came to me. If jumping up and down on the clicker could turn it on, couldn't it also turn it off?

When it came about time for Andy to come home, I attacked the clicker. Channels were changing like fury, the sound was going up and coming down but the set was still on. I started to panic, but with one lucky stroke I must have hit the right button because the picture started to shrink, make a dot and then go black.

Just at that moment Andy opened the door. I raced to meet him, wagging my tail and making him think I had another boring day. And my secret was safe!

CHAPTER NINE
"Worse Than My Bite"

Dogs bark; it's a natural thing. We're born with the ability and born with the desire. It's our thing. Leave us alone! Besides, I don't bark all the time. I usually bark when someone approaches the front door. As soon as I recognize the person, I stop. If it's Andy, the bark becomes little yelps of happiness because I am very happy to see him.

I save my loudest and most ferocious barks for the mailman (or to be P.C., I should say the mailperson.) Now since we live in an apartment, I don't see the mailperson very often. But when I do the walls of Jericho would come tumbling down again. Once in a while

Andy will get a Federal Express letter or package, and I let that carrier know that he is in for it if he tries to enter my domain. Andy always tries to shush me, but this is one time no one can stop me.

My favorite thing is to scrunch down at that little space of air between the door and floor and stick my nose right up against it. Then I bounce up and down barking at the top of my lungs. That usually scares them pretty good, and I feel as if I've earned my keep. It almost always works and they go away!

I'll bark sometimes when Andy and I are walking. If I see a really pretty little girl dog across the street, I let her know she's cute. Since I can't whistle at her (not P. C.), I bark, and she knows because all of a sudden, she'll begin to prance. Then I begin to prance to show her I know she's noticed me. Once in a while Andy will take me over to meet her, and I always like that. And of course I'm as polite as I can be except for sniffing her behind which she doesn't mind, and I don't mind, but Andy and the other dog's owner get upset about it. As I've said before, people are weird.

Then there's what I call the king-of-the-hill bark. I especially use it against very large dogs. It's a contest to see who can be more of a he-dog than the other. I'll paw the dirt; he'll paw the dirt. I'll bare my teeth; he'll bare his teeth. But nothing ever really happens. A lot of sound but no fury.

There's one more bark in my repertoire which I luckily haven't had to use. That's the "get yourself out of bed, there's an emergency" bark. I only use that if something's on fire or there's a burglar in the apartment. It's my loudest bark, and I guarantee you it will wake the dead which is about what I have to do when Andy is sleeping. I think he would sleep through the Mormon Tabernacle choir singing the "Hallelujah Chorus" in full voice. But I'm ready if I ever have to use it.

And that old saying that his "bark is worse than his bite" is, I'm afraid, very true in my case. When it comes to biting people, I'm a wimp.

CHAPTER TEN
"Cocktails for Two or Twenty"

One thing I've found about myself over the years is that I am very gregarious. I love people. I love to sniff them on the street; I love to meet them in a store; I love it when Andy has them over to the apartment for cocktails or dinner.

Andy doesn't entertain that much; he's about average, I guess. But when he does, he puts out a good spread. And he's a good cook when he's having people in for dinner. Between the two, I think cocktail parties are my favorite.

I like to weave in and out among all the people laughing and talking in the living room. Also, at a cocktail party people drop a lot more food than they do at dinner. Dinner is real work, but a cocktail party is a piece of cake, or maybe I should say a piece of paté.

I've also found that when people are having cocktails, they become a lot less inhibited. Which translated for me means they feed me more food. Andy always scolds them when he catches them doing it so I try to stay on the other side of the room from Andy when I'm choosing my quarry.

Women are my best shot. One of them will lean down and pat my head, squish her mouth and say, "Oh what a cutesy-wootsie little doggie-poo."

Do you have any idea how that makes me feel? Here I am, an adult male dog, being talked to like some two week old puppy. But I know that if I stay calm, hang my little pink tongue out and cock my head to one side, I'll get results. My batting average is about 80% when I do that. So I do it a lot.

My favorite foods are shrimp and crudités. Don't ask me why a dog should love shrimp and raw vegetables, but that's the way it is with me. Carrots are my favorite, and I love it when Andy serves carrot sticks. I make myself particularly cute when one of the guests is eating the carrots; they usually get the picture and slip me one. The shrimp are harder to come by. I mean who feeds a dog shrimp? They're almost too expensive for people, and people always want to save them for themselves. But once in a while, there's a shrimp dropped, and before you can say "What's Up, Doc?", guess who's wolfing it down? Moi!

I'm not too keen on the dips although in a crunch I'll snack on a little onion dip and Fritos. Now Fritos are something I really like. All that crunch and all that salt. It does a dog's heart good - though actually it doesn't do a dog's or a human's heart good, but who can resist?

I just have one real problem about a cocktail party or even a dinner party for that matter. There is one comfortable wing chair in the living room that is mine. I know it doesn't have my name on it, but Andy knows it's mine and I know it's mine so that should be enough.

When people come to visit, invariably someone will go sit in my chair. I can't really blame them because it's the most comfortable one in the room, but where am I supposed to sit or lie down? On the floor? How degrading!

But all is not lost because I do have a solution that I've used a number of times. At some point in the evening, the person sitting in my chair is going to get up. No matter where I am in the room, I always keep one eye trained on my chair, and the minute I see that it's empty, I race to it, jump up in it, settle down and I dare anyone to try to move me. If anyone tries, my growl is usually enough to back them off. Besides, Andy knows how sensitive I am about my chair so he usually comes to my aid and jokingly gets the person to sit somewhere else. I mean whose apartment is this, anyway?

At a dinner party, I have to be subtle. Andy has made it very clear that he won't tolerate my begging at the table. And I agree with

43

him; it's very demeaning to my self-esteem. So what I usually do is spot the best prospect and go lie down by his or her chair at the dining room table. If I'm not getting anywhere, I'll shift around a bit and try to rub up against his or her leg to remind the person that a little gray friend is in need. Sometimes it takes a little while, but usually my target gets the picture fairly quickly, and a morsel of chicken or steak will be stealthily forthcoming. I chew very quietly so Andy won't know. I think my provider appreciates that which usually means a couple of more morsels before the dinner is over.

A dog cannot live by dog food alone - especially when there's all that good human food available.

CHAPTER ELEVEN
"These Paws Were Made for Walking"

If there is one thing other than food that I live for, it's my walks. Long walks; short walks; any kind of walk that I can get, I take. With certain exceptions which you're going to hear about shortly.

A walk is my window on the world. It's the only time I can really find out what's going on outside the apartment. Sometimes that's good and sometimes that's bad. But, hey, that's life!

Andy is funny about my walks. In the morning, he always has me wait until he makes a pot of coffee so that when we walk, he has a mug of coffee to sip on for himself. That's okay with me because I don't really like coffee. Also, he's usually so sleepy that we have a really nice slow walk, and I get to sniff and poke around every smell all the way around the block.

But on those days when Andy doesn't wake up on time, he really tries to get me to walk fast, and I don't get nearly enough sniffing time. That makes me upset, and I try to hold my ground when he starts to pull me away from a new smell. I mean, if I don't get my smells, my day is like a day without sunshine.

Then there are the days when Andy takes me down to the front door of our apartment building, and I look out and see the rain pouring down. That's when I put on brakes. These paws were not meant to get wet! Andy pulls and tugs, and I pull and tug in the opposite direction. There is no way I'm going out. Finally, Andy will stop pulling and look at me. He usually says, "Okay, but it's going to be a long wait till your next walk." As if that would make me want to get soaked and have to spend the day like a used wet mop. No thanks.

Now the snow is another matter. I love the snow; it's like being showered with tiny feathers that pop when they hit you. I know you get wet from snow just like rain, but it's really different. The only bad thing is when the supers or handymen from the buildings put that rock salt on the sidewalk. They get in my paws and really hurt. No matter how hard I try, I can't always avoid them.

Andy noticed this and must have decided to do something about it whether I liked it or not. And I have to tell you, I was not a happy puppy when I saw what he had done. He bought me a red and

46

blue coat to wear in the snow and little red leather booties that tied around my legs. I was mortified. I'm not a poodle. What did he think I had a permanent fur coat for if it wasn't to keep warm!

I have to confess I resisted letting him put that coat on me the first time he tried. And if you thought that was resisting, you should have seen him try to get those boots over my paws. As he would tie one, I would turn around and untie it while he was trying to do up another one. We must have been at it for nearly an hour when Andy got really stern with me. "Buster," he said in the gruffest voice I had ever heard him use, "you're going to put these on. I spent a lot of money on these things, and you're going to wear them so you might as well get used to them now."

Well, what was I supposed to do? I do love him, and I could see I was making him unhappy. So I gave in and let him finish "dressing" me.

When we got to the street, I looked all around hoping no one would see me. The coast looked clear, and we didn't meet anyone on the block. But as we turned the corner, there was that apricot colored poodle who was always so uppity whenever she saw me. She pretended not to notice me, but as she passed me on the street, I heard her whisper low "You'll never make it as a runway model, honey", and she walked away quickly before I could nip her. And who wanted to be a runway model in the first place? It was probably her dream, and she had failed so now she was taking it out on me.

We got back home without too much more incident, and I was really relieved to be able to take off my booties and my coat.

47

The only thing to do now was to pray for sunshine. If there is a sun god, his ears must be burning now!

CHAPTER TWELVE
"Man's Best Friend"

It was a really crisp day in mid-December approaching Christmas when Andy and I set out for one of our usual walks. Andy had bought me one of those doggie coats for the cold weather, but I refused to be induced into wearing that silly thing. Besides, it wasn't that cold and it wasn't snowing or sleeting or anything like that. We walked along our usual route, but then Andy decided to add a few blocks to our trip and turned down a street which I don't think we had

49

ever been on before. There were a lot of trees along the sidewalk which made it really pleasant for us.

We had gone about two or three blocks when there in front of us huddled up against the stoop of a brownstone was what appeared to be a person covered in a lot of old sheets or blankets - I couldn't really tell exactly. As we came closer to the bundle, the top of the covers pushed back and the face of a man appeared and looked at us.

His eyes were so sad, his mouth drooped and he must have had a two week growth of beard. Also, his face was emaciated and drawn. For a moment he seemed to be deep in thought.

He looked directly at me which made me feel very uncomfortable and I thought of all the comforts of my life - my wonderful apartment, the food served to me with love, the warmth of my home and best of all my wonderful Andy. What more could a dog have to be thankful for. And here was this human being living in a condition like this on the street, in the cold, in one of the richest cities in the world about to observe its most glorious holiday - Christmas. Somehow, it seemed so wrong, and I was ashamed although I knew there was nothing I could really do to change the world. If the wag of my stub tail could help, I would gladly do it.

I wasn't sure, but I thought I saw a faint smile on his face when he looked at me, and there was a flicker of life in his eyes. Then he said to me "Hello, little fella. Cold enough for you?"

He looked up at Andy. "Would you let me give him a little pat? It's been so long since I've had a dog, but I really do love them. It'd be kinda hard for me to have one right now."

I could see that this was the last thing Andy expected to hear, and it took him a minute to answer. "If Buster is willing, that would be fine."

Wouldn't you know it. Pass the buck. But I rose to the occasion and wagged my tail and cocked my head at the man which indicated that my answer was "yes". Andy loosened up on my leash and I walked over to him.

He was very careful as he lifted his arm out of his blankets toward me. I guess he really did know that some dogs don't want you to thrust your arm or hand in front of them all of a sudden. He slowly moved his hand toward me very low with the back of his hand up so I would know he wasn't going to hit me, and he let me sniff his hand first.

I have to tell you I almost gagged because the stench was overwhelming. And yet I didn't let that bother me because I knew he didn't have anyone like Andy to bathe him or even to send him to a place where he could take a bath. He slowly turned his hand and put it under my chin and whiskers and began slowly to rub under my chin. How could he have known that was almost my favorite thing in the world!

He continued the rubbing for a minute or so and then slid his hand up to the top of my head and began patting it and slowly massaging my ears. Heaven! I wonder if he knew that rubbing a Schnauzers ears is the most soothing and relaxing thing that anyone could do. If I could have spoken I would have shouted out, "Don't stop. Ever!"

51

The man looked up at Andy. "You have a very nice dog. You're very lucky, you know."

"I know. He's my best friend."

"What a wonderful thing to have - a best friend." Andy looked at him with a caring look.

"No, no, I didn't mean for you to feel sorry for me. I've had many good things in my life before this."

"I didn't mean to make you uncomfortable. I'm sorry."

"Don't worry about it. I'll manage. I have for the past eight months."

Andy shifted a little uncomfortably. I don't think the man noticed, but I was certainly aware of it. "On the street?"

"Not always. Many times I found a shelter for a night or two."

"Why aren't you at a shelter now?"

"I don't want to wear out my welcome, and besides, there are a lot of other people who need their help as much as I do so I don't want to be hoggish about it."

I decided to look up at him and wag my tail in hopes of cheering him up. It worked because as I gazed lovingly into his eyes, he began to smile. His smile was so infectious that I could see that it was also affecting Andy who began to smile as well.

Andy said, "I hope you'll let me do something for you for Christmas."

"You don't have to do anything. Just give me a 'Merry Christmas' and I'll be fine."

"Sorry, that's not enough. But I do give you a 'Merry

Christmas' and I do mean it." With that Andy took out his wallet and emptied whatever bills he had and handed them to the man. "Please do me the honor of accepting this. It's not a lot but maybe it will bring a little comfort to you."

At first the man didn't reach for the money. So I ran up to him and nuzzled him a couple of times so that he had to put his hand out again, and I guess he must have realized my motive. He looked at me and smiled. "You win, Buster." He held out his hand and took the money. "God bless you and give you the most wonderful Christmas you've ever had."

Andy's eyes got teary. "Thank you. I think Buster and I are going to have a great time this year. And we won't forget you."

He picked himself and his bundle of covers and possessions and again smiled at us. "I won't say good-bye because I don't like the word. I know a little French and they have a wonderful expression for the way I feel: au plaisir de vous revoir. That means 'until I have the pleasure of seeing you again'." With that he was off down the street. I looked at Andy, and I have never been prouder of anyone in my whole life.

CHAPTER THIRTEEN
"To Sleep, Perchance to Dream"

I don't know exactly what it was - maybe some kind of primal urge - but I knew from the beginning I was going to have to stake out my territory for sleeping arrangements.

On my first night there, Andy had put a small box which contained a couple of soft towels on the floor in his bedroom. He took me over to the box and placed me in it, saying "good night, sleep tight" as he crawled into his king size bed with all the blankets and quilts on it.

What to do? Andy liked to sleep with the window open, which

I'm told is very healthy, but isn't fair when he has all the covers. So I decided I had to let Andy know right away that a box was not a bed.

What would be the best way to get his attention? To make sure he couldn't go to sleep! I began to cry just a little. I was ashamed to do this, but when you're desperate, you'll try anything. And it worked. Andy came over to me and petted me. He told me that everything was going to be alright and to go to sleep.

I pretended to try to do just that, but as soon as he got back in bed, I began to cry some more. After getting out of bed two or three times, Andy was beginning to get the picture.

"You want to sleep with me, don't you?" he asked.

Of course I couldn't answer him, but I licked his hand. That did it; he lifted me up into the bed with him and placed me on the pillow next to him. "Now go to sleep. But don't think you're going to be allowed to do this every night. It's just until you get used to your new home." Andy was trying to be so logical.

"Bah!" I said to myself. "Now that I'm here, he'll never get rid of me." And I soon began to snore softly which was okay because Andy snored loud and hard.

For the next several nights Andy tried the old box routine, but I was having none of it. Each time Andy would pick me up and put me in the bed on the pillow next to him. Andy liked to sleep on his side a lot so I found a very cozy spot to curl into right where he doubled himself over. And that became my permanent place to enjoy a long, peaceful night of rest.

Except when Andy turned over. I had to keep a sixth sense

going all night long because when he turned, it was kind of violent. If I wasn't careful, I could get squashed, which almost happened a couple of times, but each time I was able to crawl away at the last moment out of harm's way. But when he got back to sleep, I always managed to find a place to curl into for the rest of the night.

Then the unthinkable occurred. Andy was having someone stay over for the night which meant that my bed was going to be taken over by someone else. I fought this as hard as possible. When Andy would put me down, I jumped right back up and settled in between the two pillows and dared anyone to move me. This is when I really developed my growl factor.

But it was no use. After I had been put down two or three times, Andy picked me up and put me outside of the bedroom and closed the door. This was going too far! He knew I couldn't open a doorknob. What was I to do? Then I remembered: "if he can't sleep because of the noise I make, I win".

At first I decided to scratch the door. This made a very annoying sound, and soon there was Andy standing in the doorway looking angry and saying things like "no" and "bad dog". All this abuse because I was trying to exercise my domiciliary rights!

Next, I tried the crying routine again. I knew this was effective, but somehow Andy didn't react. So I got louder and louder. At last there was Andy again. I'm not sure what he was preparing to do, but I heard the voice of Andy's friend say "let him in; it's okay with me".

Andy picked me up and took me back to the bed where I

settled in between the two pillows. I had proved my point that this bed was mine, too, and couldn't be taken away from me. I dreamed all night about chasing rabbits and squirrels.

Oh, joy; oh, rapture!

CHAPTER FOURTEEN
"Time"

I am an animal who is used to a routine, and I really hate it when my routine is interrupted. Don't get me wrong - I love Andy, but sometimes I get very put out about the way he doesn't follow the rules.

I suppose I ought to be more tolerant because he does work long hours, and I'm sure he works very hard doing whatever it is that he does. But I have needs too. And one of the most important is that I need to have my walk when it's time for my walk, and I need to eat when it's time for me to eat.

I do confess that Andy is pretty good about all of that. But once in a while I find myself waiting for him when he's supposed to be there, and he isn't. That's when my stomach starts to growl at me.

What if something's happened to him? Did he forget about me? Was he kidnaped? All these horrible ideas race through my mind. What can I do?

I don't know how to use the telephone; I can't cry out for help. I guess I could bark, but that would only upset the nosy neighbor if she's in the hallway, and she'd begin yelling at me to shut up all that barking or she's going to call the pound.

I'll be stuck here with no food and no walks. Not only will I be starving, but this apartment is going to be a disaster area. Where are you, Andy?

Then the practical side of things starts to rear its ugly head. I really need to go for a walk! The first thing I do is try not to think about it. I start counting backwards from 99, but since I don't know really how to count, that doesn't do any good. I try to think of beautiful things, but every beautiful thing turns into a crashing waterfall or gushing river, and that just makes things worse. Sleep seems to be the only answer.

I go to one of my favorite spots for sleeping during the day - in the closet behind Andy's clothes. I guess it's a throwback to the days when my ancestors lived in the woods and slept in caves because that spot really is like a cave. It's dark, it's warm and it's safe. But this is when I find out what insomnia is all about. I lie on my side; I turn over onto my back; I spread out with my paws out in front and my legs out in back. Nothing helps. All I can think about is trees, bushes

60

and fire hydrants.

Please, God, let him come home right now and give his best friend the walk he so desperately needs. I try crossing my legs really tight, and strangely enough, this seems to help. But how long can I stay in that position? It isn't really very comfortable. But I 'm determined to succeed.

Then I hear footsteps in the hall. At last! I come out of my cave and race to the front door, but the steps go on by, and I realize they weren't Andy's steps at all. I'm getting thirsty, but I know better than to drink any water. That's just piling it on.

Since I can't tell time on the clock, I don't actually know what time it is, but one thing I do know is that it's way past the time Andy should be at home. And he isn't here.

Then just as I'm getting really despondent, I hear the elevator door open. I don't know how I know it, but I do know it. Andy's getting off that elevator. And then the familiar steps down the hall. And none too soon. The key turns, the door opens and there's Andy looking down at me.

"Buster, did you miss me?" What a stupid remark.

Andy closes the door behind him, not a good sign. He heads to the bathroom. "Just a minute. I have to go and then we'll walk."

I can't believe he could be so inconsiderate. I'm the one who's been holding it in all day. But then I realize that we'll really be going out shortly, and so I run to the water bowl and lap up as much as I can hold.

Andy comes in with my leash. "You drank a lot of water,

Buster. I guess we'd better take our walk now." Andy isn't a rocket scientist.

I lift my neck up while Andy fastens the leash to my collar and pray to God that someday Andy will get the fact that even though I'm not a Virgo, I still need my schedule.

CHAPTER FIFTEEN
"Are You What You Eat?"

There's an old wives' tale which has been around a long time, as most old wives' tales have been, which says that a Schnauzer will eat himself to death if given the opportunity. And like most old wives' tales, this one is true also. I don't personally know any Schnauzers who have eaten themselves to death, but that's because living in an apartment in New York, I don't get the opportunity to meet too many other Schnauzers and certainly none who has eaten himself to death.

We do love to eat. And we're really not that particular. However, I have to tell you a few things I won't eat: raw mushrooms (taste like cardboard); ginger (I'm not a Shar Pei); coffee (although if it has enough cream in it, I might get a little down); celery (I eat it but it sticks between my teeth); and escargots (maybe I would if I were a French poodle, Heaven forbid!).

When I was just a little tyke (i.e. eight weeks old) when Andy brought me to his home to live, the only food I got was from the supermarket and marketed as "dog food". Some of it came in cans and some of it came in bags. I guess someone told Andy to mix and match because I usually got half "wet" (i.e. canned) food and half dry (i.e. "bagged") food. Andy wanted me to eat only this dog food, but I trained him pretty quickly to let me taste what he was eating. My big, brown eyes, slightly moist with desire, always won him over, and soon I was dining on Andy's elegant meals: slices of pizza, remnants of Big Macs, bagels with cream cheese and lox, leftover Chinese (I but always avoid those little red peppers-they are hot!), day-old pasta, etc. I ate like a king!

But then one day it all stopped. Andy must have consulted a health-food guru because all the goodies dried up, and all I began to see were fruits and vegetables and very lean chicken. There was also fish, but since I'm not a cat, that really didn't interest me. But Andy ate a lot of it. Suddenly, life became very boring if I may speak culinarily, and I realized I had to take things into my own hands if I was ever going to taste something good again. Something with fat; something with salt. Is that too much to ask? I don't think so.

Since my area of travel was pretty small and I knew there would be nothing that I wanted in Andy's apartment, my only other choice was the street. I have to admit that I had noticed an interesting smell or two before on walks, but since I was getting good stuff at home, I basically ignored their call. I knew what I had to do.

It just so happened that on an evening walk I was particularly feeling the need for something to taste a few bites of New York cuisine. My sense of smell was on red-alert for anything that might give me a taste sensation.

I walked very slowly which I'm sure made Andy think something was up so I knew that I had to be especially sneaky if I was going to retrieve any "goodie" of value. But if I walked too fast, then I was sure to miss any number of morsels to snack on.

We came to the big tree which I loved and which had a lot of ground cover around it. The perfect place to find a scrap if there was one to be found! I walked casually into the grass and over to the tree with my nose to the ground, hoping for a bonanza. Maybe some deep-fried chicken or part of a burger with secret sauce. A piece of chocolate from a Hershey bar or a Reese's Pieces bit were whirling around as possibilities in my brain. But nothing! Nada! Nein! In any language I was out of luck.

As we started walking down the street again, I saw a friend and neighbor of Andy's walking toward us. I realized this would be a perfect opportunity for me if there was anything to be found. I sped up just a bit to get to the next grassy area which I managed to reach at the same time as Andy's friend reached us. As he said "hello" to Andy, I wagged my tail especially hard which got him to reach down and pet me and also to cause him to stop so that he and Andy could get into a conversation as they often did. It worked, and I was left to my own devices. Exactly what I wanted!

What was that which I saw before me? A very nice chunk of pizza crust with a little sauce and a touch of cheese still on it. I couldn't tell how old it was, but it seemed fine. After taking a quick glance to see that Andy wasn't looking, I scooped the crust into my mouth with the stealth of a CIA agent, chewed quickly and quietly a couple of times and then down the gullet.

A few more quick sniffs and with my nose moving the grass around at will, I uncovered a couple of salted peanuts (salt and fat all in one package) and some skin from a KFC (I assumed) chicken which was SO recently put there that it was almost warm. Just as I got this into my mouth Andy saw me and yelled out "Drop it, Buster!"

I pretended I was waiting for a bus and paid no attention to him. Just as he reached down to take it out of my mouth, I swallowed. Just in time. One more second and he would have had it, but he didn't.

"Bad dog," Andy said to me. "You know you don't eat things from the street."

Was he kidding? I knew no such thing. I knew that he told me not to eat from the street, but that's a far cry from my knowing that I didn't eat things from the street. A lot of semantics, but it was all I needed to justify my actions. I looked up at him with my best guilty look on my face, and he melted as he always did. "It's too late now, but promise me you won't do it again." Now Andy thinks I can't speak "human" so that was a ridiculous statement, but since I couldn't speak, I didn't have to promise anything.

Andy's friend said good-bye and we began walking again with Andy keeping a very sharp eye out for me so I realized that it would be best not to try anything more for the time being.

But as someone once said, "Tomorrow is another day!"

CHAPTER SIXTEEN
"East is East"

There are lots of Hamptons in New York. There's Southampton, Westhampton, Hampton Bays and, as Andy and his friends say, the only Hampton that counts - East Hampton. So when it came time for Andy and his friends to rent that little weekend hide-away for the summer, East Hampton was the choice.

I didn't go out with Andy the weekend they went looking for a place. But I know when he and a couple of his friends got back that night, they were very excited and couldn't stop talking about the place they rented and what a bargain it was. They really got my curiosity up, but. I knew I'd see it before long.

They had been lucky and had gotten the house beginning the first weekend in May rather than Memorial Day which was the more usual time for a summer rental to begin. But they had been told that the owners were going to be out of the country anyway so they could have the extra time for free.

My personal opinion when I saw the place was that there weren't any owners. The place was a shack and not even a good one. No wonder they got a "steal" except they were the ones who were stolen from I think.

The living room was kind of small. The only furniture were a hard wooden couch with a couple of throw pillow on it, two wooden chairs and a table with ice cream parlor chairs around it. I guessed that must be the dining table. But it did have a television set even though it was black & white. But Andy said he had an extra one which he would bring out next time.

There were three bedrooms for six people so it meant doubling up in every room. One had bunk beds, and the other two had single beds that looked like left over World War II surplus. And they all had chenille bedspreads on them. Thank goodness Andy wasn't in a bunk bed. What if he'd had the top bunk? It was too unnerving to even think about. I really don't like heights.

The worst of all was that there was only one bathroom for six people. They all joked about it, but no one seemed to care. This was just for weekends and roughing it would be fun and it was cheap and all that. I thought they were just making jokes to cover up what had obviously been a big mistake made in the heat of the moment.

And then I found out we weren't really in East Hampton after all but in a place called Three Mile Harbor. Of course, everyone still referred to it as East Hampton, but I knew it wasn't.

The one really good thing about the property was that it had a nice piece of land around it, and I quickly noticed that there weren't any fences so maybe I could do a little exploring this summer. Andy must have read my mind because he made everyone in the house swear they wouldn't let me go out alone, and if I went out, it had to be on a leash. "Rats!" as Snoopy would say. Oh, yes, Andy read "Peanuts" to me ever so often, especially when Snoopy was making a good joke. But he couldn't really think that I would fall for the idea that a dog could talk to birds. That's ridiculous.

Neither Andy nor any of his friends had cars so they went out to the house via the Hampton Jitney (shuttle van) or on the Long Island Railroad. The railroad was my favorite because the only way Andy could take me was in the parlor car. And compared to regular coach, the parlor car was heaven! I could sit in Andy's lap all the way out, and sometimes when we had a really nice person working the train, he would let me walk around the car while we were moving. Luckily we didn't have a lot of luggage because Andy had taken what he needed for the summer out to the house on the first weekend.

By the second weekend we were there, it had become obvious to everybody that we had to have a car, nothing fancy, but something to get us around. And they found an ad in the paper for a used car for $300 which meant $50 per person. There was a lot of skepticism as to

71

whether the car would even run, but sure enough it did, and even though it looked like a reject from a junkyard, it got us around.

It was really fun to go to town. The town of East Hampton is very beautiful and very charming. It isn't big, but it has great shops and very smart-looking people. And, of course their dogs had as much attitude as the people did. But even though they went into their "my owner is more important than your owner" mode with me, I didn't let them get away with it. I told them all that I was a Disney star, and they couldn't disprove it since dogs weren't allowed into the movie house. So there!

I must say I really didn't like being in the country every weekend. The house was empty except for me during the day because the household usually went to the beach. And at night there were so many people that I had to be careful not to get stepped on. Also, when we were there on the weekend, Andy hardly had any time at all for me. I understood, I guess, but I didn't appreciate it. After all, I am his best friend.

CHAPTER SEVENTEEN
"A Marriage of Inconvenience"

Through most of the history of civilization the marriage of a daughter or son has been arranged by the parents. It's only in recent times that the concept of "love" has been allowed to be a part of the marriage game. Well, that's for humans.

For us dogs the marriage is still arranged! Andy got it into his head that it would be a good idea to have me meet a nice female schnauzer and have puppies so he could get the pick of the litter and give it to his sister in Houston, Texas. Did I have a choice? Did I have a voice? No!

This little female, whose name was Molly, was owned by

some friends of Andy's. Molly and Buster! What a combination to start a line of champions! Anyway, they settled all the details, and I was taken by Andy down to his friends' apartment in the Village. I met Molly, and she was a really cute young thing, but she didn't show much interest in me when we met. There was also a large gray and white cat in the apartment which I thought might be fun to terrorize when Andy left.

Andy and his friends talked, but I could tell they were looking sideways at Molly and me as often as they dared. Molly didn't have much to say, and she didn't seem particularly friendly, as I said, so I decided to just plop myself down on the rug and rest. This was apparently not what all the human folk had intended. Andy came over, picked me up and took me over to Molly again. What could I do if she didn't want to socialize? But for Andy's sake, I tried again, still without much luck.

Andy's friend, Delia, said that it would probably be best if I stayed at their apartment for a day or two until I got to know Molly better and vice-versa. I didn't like that suggestion one little bit. I ran over to Andy and curled up by his foot with one paw over his shoe so I'd be sure he understood that I was going to leave with him. But they discussed it for a few minutes, and I knew Andy was going to give in.

I was so depressed after Andy left that I just curled up and tried to go to sleep. I'd forgotten all about terrorizing the cat, whose name was Maude. I guess they liked the "M" words. But Maude hadn't forgotten about me. She came nosing up to see if I was really asleep.

I guess she somehow knew how depressed I was, and instead of bothering me, she curled up beside me to give me comfort. I thought that was the nicest thing that had happened to me all day so I just stayed right there next to her. Besides, Molly was still being aloof.

The next day Andy's friends went to work, leaving the three of us alone. Maude was amazing! She climbed onto the sofa and then walked across the back of it like a trained acrobat. From there she leaped onto a table full of all sorts of things and managed not to break anything or even knock anything out of place. She continued on around the room in this fashion until I was in complete awe. If she was showing off for my sake, it worked.

I thought I'd see if I could do the same thing. I climbed onto the sofa and got onto the top and began walking but quickly fell off. Like that spider that Robert the Bruce saw, I tried again with the same result. Then I decided to take it more slowly and be very careful. Voila! I walked the whole back of the sofa.

When I looked over at the table though, I knew I was beaten. I didn't believe I could jump that far, and even if I did, I knew I would cause everything to come crashing to the floor. That would put me in real trouble. Maude was watching, and I could see her grin. So the grin doesn't belong only to Cheshire cats!

The more I ignored her, the more friendly Molly became. Women! I'll never figure them out. This time she came over to me. I don't know what perfume she was wearing, but something smelled very alluring. I rubbed up against her and nipped at her ear. She pretended to be annoyed, but I knew she was just being coquettish. So

I nipped again. And she nipped back.

But then for some reason she became stand-offish again. I know it wasn't anything I said because I hadn't said anything. It's just the way she is, I thought. Go with the flow. So I went over to Maude and began to play with her.

Molly was jealous. Good. It served her right. She'd better realize when she's got a good man, she'd better hang onto him. As the song says, we're hard to find.

Maude was getting bored watching Molly be so wishy-washy so she jumped up onto a shelf and curled up in the clear glass salad bowl where she could just watch proceedings without getting involved. I desperately wanted to be able to jump like that and curl up in a salad bowl, but I knew it wasn't in the cards.

Besides, Molly had now decided to flirt with me seriously. We sniffed and nipped and just when I thought we were getting somewhere, Molly would run away. At this rate I thought I'd probably have to live in that apartment for a month or two.

What was wrong with her?

We were still playing this game when Delia and Sam got home from work. From the looks on their faces I could tell they didn't think Molly and I had mated yet, and of course they were right. They called Molly over and began to pet her and stroke her. Then Sam got me and brought me over to her and they surrounded us. That wasn't the way to do it, but they didn't know.

I looked at Molly, and she looked at me. In that instance, I knew the time was right. I took Molly's lead when she left the living

76

room and went back to one of the bedrooms. And in the dark we began to nuzzle and lick, and that's when it happened.

Delia called Andy, and he came down and got me. He heaped praise on my head for being such a good boy. I didn't see any reason for all that, but if it led to a couple of extra dog biscuits, what the heck.

It was weeks and weeks later when I heard Andy yelp at the person he was talking to on the telephone. Six puppies? Really? That's great. I'll be down tomorrow. Oh? Okay, I'll wait for a couple of weeks till their eyes open and they look more like dogs."

And that's how I found out I was a papa. I confess that Andy did tell me about it after he hung the telephone up, but I thought I should have been called directly. After all, if it hadn't been for me, there wouldn't be any puppies. But people don't seem to think like that.

And you know the really rotten part? I never even got to see them. I guess it never crossed Andy's or Delia's or Sam's minds that I might want to see my children.

But like they say, it's a dog's life so you take the good with the bad.

CHAPTER EIGHTEEN
"By the Beautiful Sea"

As the week inched along toward Friday, the day we left for East Hampton, I overheard Andy on the telephone with someone. He was accepting an invitation to go somewhere, but I didn't know where or who he was talking to. Then I heard him pick up the telephone and call Phil, one of his house mates in East Hampton.

"I won't be coming out this weekend. I've been invited to go to Kismet on Fire Island. I've never been there, and it sounds like fun."

"I've been invited?" was all I could think. Not "We've been

invited" or "Buster and I have been invited", but "I've been invited". Where did this leave me? Alone in the hot city all weekend, and as everyone knows, weekend television is pretty poor. And who was going to walk me or feed me? I was feeling miserable.

But on Friday afternoon when Andy got home, he pulled out my carrying case, and I almost had a heart attack racing to the case and jumping in! I was so happy! I had been invited after all!

Fire Island. I had heard stories about it from other dogs who'd been there. It sounded neat. It was really just a big sand bar sitting off the south coast of Long Island. But I heard there was lots going on out there night and day.

Adventure!

I thought we were going to do our usual parlor car train ride, but Andy didn't tell the cabbie to go to Penn Station, he mentioned some other place that I had never heard of. We got there on the FDR Drive, and I could see a couple of airplanes sitting in the water. How strange!

Andy grabbed me and headed toward a plane. My heart was pounding. How can a plane take off if it's sitting in water?

Andy strapped himself in, let me out of my carrying case into his lap and a miracle occurred. The plane started moving in the water! We started to go faster and faster, and the next thing I knew we were in the air. My first airplane ride! I had hoped it would be on the Concorde, but this was better than nothing. I wasn't at all scared. In fact, I wanted to poke my head out of the window and let the wind fly through my eyes and ears, but the pilot didn't think that was a good idea so Andy held me back.

As we flew toward Fire Island, I could look down and see JFK Airport with all those big airplanes moving around. I looked off to the right and wanted to jump out of my skin. There was this huge plane coming straight into our line of flight. I knew we were done for. I closed my eyes and held on tight to Andy. I heard a noise, but nothing hit us, and I saw the big plane going in for a landing. I sighed a sigh of relief (yes, dogs can get anxious, too, you know!)

There ahead of us was Fire Island. It was so long I couldn't see all the way to the end of it. And it was so narrow. I knew I could run across it in less than three minutes.

It was covered with houses.

We started coming in for the landing and were heading straight for the water. I reasoned that if it could take off from the water, it must be able to land on the water. And I was right. The landing was smooth, and the pilot taxied in as far as he could. He apologized for having to let us out into the water.

I was itching to get out of the plane and onto dry land. Andy got out first and sank chest deep into the water. It was high tide! What a disaster. There was no way he could carry me in my case in water that deep so he put me under one arm and carried my case and his bag in the other hand. Slowly we waded to shore. I have to confess I was twitching mightily because I could feel the water lapping under me, and I was sure I was going to get my baptism right then and there. My Andy, my hero, made it in safely without my getting a drop of water on me.

81

The people in the house were nice, but there were an awful lot of them. We had to sleep on a side porch which was screened in so it wasn't bad. And as I've told you, Andy loves fresh air so he was fine about it.

I guess the main reason everybody loves Fire Island is the beach because that's where everyone went for the whole day on Saturday and Sunday. I had seen the beach in East Hampton, but the people there didn't seem as frantic about it as they did on Fire Island. It was almost like a ritual or worship.

Sam and Delia were there with Molly, but Molly pretended she had never met me. I don't mean she was rude - just standoffish. I couldn't understand her attitude after all we had been to each other, but I was concentrating on having a good time. I hoped I would be asked to go to the beach.

My dream came true! Andy took a bowl and some water (and of course dog biscuits) and a big umbrella. I think there were about ten of us trooping to the water like the baby turtles on the Galapagos Islands (I saw it on TV). Molly didn't come. I guess Sam and Delia thought she was too delicate.

When we got to the end of the walk, we stepped down onto the sand. "Ouch! Ouch! Ouch!" was all I could say to myself. The sand was hot, and my little paws weren't used to that kind of blistering surface. Andy noticed my plight and quickly picked me up until we got to the spot where we would claim our space.

The first thing Andy did was to set up the umbrella so I'd have shade to sit in. A fur coat really isn't proper beachwear, but what could

I do? It doesn't unzip. Besides, I saw pictures on TV of all those women in Miami decked out in fur coats in ninety degree weather. Now I knew how they must suffer for vanity.

The whole group threw their things down and began racing toward the water. Andy called to me to come with them, so hot sand and all I raced alongside Andy. Then I saw where they were going. Huge waves of water were swirling out there and then coming toward me on the shore. The moment I saw one start to come in, I backed up quickly. Andy called to me, "Don't be afraid. It's only water. It can't hurt you."

I've already told you about me and water, and the rain is nothing compared to those masses of water-filled waves that Andy and his friends seemed to thrive on. I just looked at them for a moment, and then had to decide whether to go back to the umbrella or to explore.

I found that the sand closer to the water was cooler so I stayed on that without letting the waves get to me. Then I saw two people beckoning me to come to them. Well, why not? They were two very pretty girls in their twenties. Maybe they had food. They patted me on the head, said "Nice doggie" but didn't offer me any goodies for my trouble. I started to go, but one of the girls held me by the collar.

"Don't run away. We want you to stay with us."

I didn't like the sound of that and tried to wiggle away, but she was holding firm. Frantically, I looked for Andy but couldn't see him. I was getting frightened. What did these girls intend to do, take me with them? I could never let that happen. They held me captive for about ten minutes which had me very worried. Then I saw them packing up to leave, and they hadn't let me go.

Just at that moment I saw Andy running down the beach. In my loudest voice used for fires and burglars, I barked and barked until Andy looked over and saw me. He came running over to me and in picking me up, loosened the girl's grip on my collar.

"Were you trying to run away?" he teased me. I tried to give my best impression of a "no" answer.

One of the girls spoke up. "We didn't know who he belonged to so we were just keeping him safe." What a liar! They were out to dognap me, and I knew it.

Andy played it cool. "Thanks so much." With that we turned and left. A narrow escape.

When we got back to the umbrella I was very relieved, very thirsty and very hot from the sun. My basic instinct took hold, and I began to dig. Somehow I knew that if I dug deep enough, there would be cool sand waiting for me. All the generations of schnauzer know-how went into my task, and the sand was flying out from behind me. Unfortunately, there were people sitting next to us who didn't appreciate what I was doing. Andy had to restrain me, and he helped me dig till I got the cool sand I wanted. Andy dug a hole and put my water bowl into it next to me, and, I was in heaven. I spent the rest of the day observing what human beings do on the beach.

All in all, I think I got the best deal.

CHAPTER NINETEEN
"Puppy Love"

I nearly always manage to make every day of my life a happy day. While Andy was at work during the day, I wandered around the apartment examining all of Andy's treasures (as well as trash), found a patch of sunshine in which to lie and bask and generally have a good time.

Into each life, as they say, a little rain must fall. But why did mine have to be a monsoon?

Andy brought his friend Brick over to the apartment after work for a drink. I, of course, stayed in the living room with them since I wanted to catch up on everything that was happening in the world, and I knew that Brick was so bright that he'd tell Andy everything.

They talked about politics and show business and stuff like that, and then came the bombshell. In a very casual and offhand way Andy said to Brick, "I'm thinking about getting a new puppy."

My hair stood on end; my blood raced; my heart pounded!

This couldn't be true! My friend was betraying me, and doing it so casually. Did he think I had no feelings?

And then he rubbed salt into the wound. "I'm doing it for Buster. I know it must be lonely for him when I'm gone all day."

Lonely? I had the soaps; I had the talk shows and game shows; I had the joy of exploring every nook and cranny of the apartment. Lonely? No! Bored? Maybe a little, but basically no! He's using me as a scapegoat. He just wants another little puppy, and now that I'm a grown dog, he doesn't have the same feelings for me. Life is so cruel.

I buried my face in my paws and didn't move. Brick looked over to where I was lying and said to Andy, "Buster seems sad."

"Oh, no, he's just resting. Why should he be sad to have a new playmate?" Andy still didn't get it.

My mind was racing to try to think of some way to stop this travesty. How could I make him aware that I didn't want anyone else in the apartment. It belonged to him and me, and we didn't need a third party. Oh, sometimes I wish I could just shout it out in English rather than use doggie tricks to try to get a message across. The only thing I could think of doing at that moment was to go back into the bedroom and crawl under the bed. I didn't want to hear any more.

After Brick finally left, Andy came back to the bedroom to get me, but I had decided to punish him for his treachery. "Come on, Buster, everything's going to be alright," Andy whispered.

"Hah!" is all I could think of. I stayed put.

Andy got down on his all fours and looked under the bed and again coaxed me to come out. Still I refused. Then he went back to the kitchen and brought two juicy dog biscuits into the bedroom to tempt me. I have to confess that I do have a weakness for those biscuits, and besides, I was tired of playing the martyr so out I came. But only after Andy promised to take me with him to the pet store.

Together we went back to the store where Andy had found me. Déjà vu all over again! I had forgotten how much I hated the place. But the owner came up to us and told Andy what a fine looking dog I had become, and of course he was right. I knew right off that he was going to use every device he could to get Andy to buy another dog. And I was going to use every trick up my beard to see that he didn't.

The first puppy that he brought out was a very light shade of gray, which I personally didn't like at all. Also, he had no personality. Andy rejected him right away without my having to get involved. Then came a little female, about eight weeks old, who was a beautiful shade of dark gray. She had those eyes that seem to be melting into themselves every time you look at her. I could see that Andy liked her. He put her down on the floor beside me, to get my approval I guess. I pretended she wasn't there and just stepped over her and moved away. Andy seemed to be very disappointed, and despite all the urging by

87

the store owner, Andy wouldn't buy her because he knew I disapproved.

The owner told Andy that he had only one Schnauzer left for him to see. It was a male, and I have to admit he was something to see - cute as a button and very frisky. I realized I might be in real trouble with that one.

Andy picked him up, and that little mutt started licking his ear! That's my trick, and he was stealing it! I could see Andy beginning to stroke him and put his face up against him just the way he had done with me. I had to do something.

When Andy bent down to put the puppy on the floor, I sneaked up behind him and nipped the puppy on the back leg. He lunged around and sank his teeth into Andy's arm which made Andy drop him and cry out in pain. "That dog is vicious," Andy told the store owner. "I'm not getting another dog today and probably not ever. You should be more careful with your dogs."

Andy turned to leave and picked me up, whispering in my ear, "I'll never find another one like you so let's just let it be me and you. What do you say?"

I turned my face up to his and licked him on the mouth, and Andy hugged me to him.

Love really does make the world go 'round.

CHAPTER TWENTY
Good Grooming?

There comes a time in the life of every dog who lives with his owner in New York City to go to the groomer. I remember very well the first time for me. I was being doused with water and soap, and all sorts of other terrible things were happening to me. How could Andy let them do this to me!

I'm sure I was very difficult that first time. I confess I was probably just as difficult the second and third times as well. And the fourth and fifth. You get the picture. At first Andy would light up with a smile and say, Buster, you're going to the cleaners today. Isn't that wonderful? Since I didn't understand what the cleaners was, I would wag my tail and look excited the way I knew he wanted me to look. And a trip was a trip, I thought. Wrong!

I caught on pretty fast what cleaners meant. The tail stopped wagging; I stopped looking eager; sometimes I would try to hide under the couch and force Andy to drag me out or bribe me out. I was still a sucker for a biscuit!

The groomer's shop was only three or four blocks away from the apartment so we always walked there. I guess I'm a cockeyed optimist, as the song says, because each time I would assure myself that we weren't going to the groomer's but just for an extra walk. Each time I was wrong.

I had learned to recognize that storefront even before Andy got me there. The front paws put on brakes; the neck stiffened; and centuries of Schnauzer hard-headedness took over. I was not going in there! I was not! Generally, Andy, after trying to drag me in, just reached down and scooped me up into his arms and carried me in. "Oh", I thought to myself at those times, "why couldn't I have been born a 'standard' Schnauzer. Then I'd like to see him try and pick me up."

Andy always said the same thing to the groomer. "Be sure to leave his feathers."

The first time I heard that I thought Andy had lost his mind. What am I? A cockatoo? A parrot? Feathers? Then one time later when Andy picked me up, he said to the groomer, "I think you've trimmed too much of his feathers." Then he grabbed my legs and started to show the groomer what he meant.

"Eureka!" I said to myself. "Feathers equals fluffy fur on my legs and chest." I agreed with Andy as I saw myself in the mirror. This time the groomer had gone too far. But he never did it again. I always came out perfect after that.

I don't want to go into all the details of the torture I'm put through just to become handsome. It's a real ordeal, and unless you've been there, you can't possibly imagine. The bath and the shaving of my fur are bad enough, but I really hate the blow dryer. It's so hot and noisy that it gets me really upset. Well, here I am going on about the details, and I said I wouldn't. But as all stories should, this one has a happy ending. Now whenever Andy comes to get me from the groomer's and we step outside onto the street, my little chest swells with pride, I have a new spring in my step and I hold my head high as I walk through the streets back home. I see my reflection from time to time in store windows as we're walking, and I know I have every reason to be proud.

I know I'm probably sounding very vain, but like Mel Brooks said, "When you've got it, flaunt it!"

92

CHAPTER TWENTY-ONE
"Going to Business"

Our routine every morning was pretty much the same. Andy would throw on some old clothes, give me a walk and feed me breakfast when we got back. Then he would have coffee and read the New York Times. When he'd finish the paper, it was shave and shower time. Then he'd put on his suit and tie and in the winter his heavy coat and go to the office, wherever that was.

But one morning, the routine changed. We didn't go for my walk the first thing. Andy had coffee and read the paper, shaved and showered, dressed and then asked me if I was ready for my walk. Was he kidding? I had been ready for an hour and was wondering what was going on.

I immediately knew that this walk would be different. We didn't turn left as we always did but turned right. My curiosity was almost at the breaking point. Then we crossed over First Avenue and kept on walking. Well, I decided just to relax and enjoy it. The new smells were intriguing; I looked for a new manhole cover to utilize; all in all it was very satisfactory.

When we got to Third Avenue we turned north and walked another three blocks and then stopped in front of this very tall building. Before I knew what was happening Andy pulled me along with him into this sumptuous marble lobby with lots of people coming and going. I started to slide on the marble because I couldn't get any traction, but gradually I found my footing. Several people looked at me and smiled, but since I couldn't smile, I didn't. But I did try to look pleasant and appreciative.

We walked over to a place which had a line of what looked like doors on both sides of the hall. One of the doors opened and I realized that they were a lot of elevators. Andy and I got into one of them with a lot of other people. The doors closed, and then I thought my heart was going to come out through I my nose. We were whizzing up, up, up. I began to feel dizzy, but just then the elevator came to a slow and easy stop, and Andy and I got out.

I was beginning to put two and two together. This is where Andy came every day to work. I wondered what he did. I looked around and saw a lot of offices and desks with people behind them. But I couldn't tell what was happening. Then I heard someone talking in a loud voice saying, "What kind of an advertising agency is this anyway? Where are the bialys? There aren't any more bialys left."

Another voice, equally loud, "Shut up, Sylvia, we haven't had bialys in the last two weeks so quit bitching." I guess Andy had heard enough. He led me to an office, which I found out was his own private one. It wasn't big, but it was very modern, and he had a lot of framed pictures of magazine ads on the wall. He had a computer on a table by his desk and a chair in front of the desk. And what a view! I ran over to the window which came all the way down to the floor. I began to back away because I couldn't tell whether I was going to fall out or not, and it looked like a long way down.

Andy took my leash off and told me he would be back in just a minute. He closed the door when he left, and there I was, the occupant of an office at an advertising agency. I wasn't really sure what Andy did for the agency, but it must be important if he had his own private office.

In a couple of minutes he came back with a cup full of water for me. I felt it would only be polite if I drank a little even though I wasn't thirsty, but since he had made the effort, I wanted him to know he was appreciated. He patted me on the head.

Just then a very beautiful and sexy young woman knocked on Andy's door and came in. She saw me and cried out, "Andy, I didn't know you had a poodle!"

The age-old dilemma 'to bite or to pee.' But I wasn't at home, and if I was bad, maybe Andy would never let me come back again so I stood still while she came over and rubbed my head and back.

95

Andy defended me. "He's a Schnauzer, not a poodle, and if he could talk, I suspect he would tell you that in no uncertain terms." Andy knew me very well.

She leaned over and chucked me under my chin. "I'm sorry. Will you forgive me?" Then she batted those long, dark lashes so how could I do anything but give her hand a lick. "He likes me," she exclaimed to Andy.

"Yes, I think he does." Just then several other people came into the room, apparently having just been told that Andy had a visitor. I was getting petted and rubbed from every direction which may sound nice but which actually isn't. Being rubbed from all directions is a little like running the gauntlet; you never know which direction it's coming from or how hard it's going to be.

I realized that all this fuss was taking Andy away from his job, and if he didn't do his job, there'd be no roof over our heads, no food on the table and no more biscuits for me. I left my crowd of admirers, walked over to Andy and curled up next to his foot. Andy smiled, "I guess that's it for now. I've got to get to work."

All the people left, Andy turned on his computer, leaned back in his chair to think and I went to sleep. What a wonderful way to spend the morning!

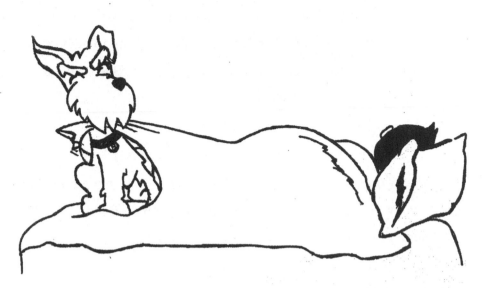

CHAPTER TWENTY-TWO
"Oh, How He Hates to Get Up"

Andy is not a morning person. I, on the other hand, am which makes for a difficult situation sometimes. Not during the Monday through Friday week because Andy knows he has to go to his job. But Saturday and Sunday are something else. Since I don't read, it's hard for me to know Tuesday from Saturday which can create quite a conflict in my home. I figure it's part of my job to help the getting-up-in-the-morning impaired to wake sufficiently to realize they have to leave the arms of Morpheus and come back to the real world. Like Oscar Wilde's coward, I do it with a kiss. Or, more accurately, several kisses.

The first kiss is always the ear lick. This usually gets Andy to squirming just a little. Then I try a second. More squirming. Then I work on the area under his ear and down onto the neck. By this time his eyes may or may not be open. The one sure way to get him active is to lick him on the lips. I love it; Andy doesn't. But I have to say it gets him up every time. He always tells me not to do that ever again, but I know he doesn't mean it.

The nice thing about morning is that when I finally get him awake, we play tussle or hide-and-seek. He'll toss me around on the bed a few times, and I growl menacingly at him, but of course I don't mean a growl of it. Then he'll put one of his hands under the covers and slowly move toward me. I stand there until he gets right up to me, and then I pounce. He's pretty quick though, and it's often hard to get him. I've discovered his secret, though. When he starts moving under the covers, I attack his shoulder because I know it's attached to his arm and hand even if he doesn't think I know that. It always makes him laugh.

The weekends, however, are different. As I said, since I don't know one day from another, I do my usual kissing and licking routine on Saturday just as I do on all other days. But this time he puts a pillow over his head so I can't get to him. I frankly don't know how he breathes under that pillow. But somehow he manages.

Then I try to snuggle under the covers to attack him from a different angle. That's not always so easy since when he tosses at night, he tends to wrap himself in the sheets and blanket. If this doesn't work, then I wait for my moment to make my next move.

I guess it eventually gets too hot for him under the pillow, and part of his face will become exposed. Just my luck!

Slowly I sneak over to him, find a vulnerable spot and move in. This always gets Andy annoyed, and he pushes me off the bed.

Some nerve, pushing me off my own bed!

I go into the living room and lie down on the rug. I try not to think that it's a way past my morning walk time. Sometimes I have to cross my legs so I don't feel the urge as much. If I can manage to get back to sleep, the time passes quickly, and suddenly there's Andy dressed in his old clothes and ready to give me a walk. All is forgiven.

I'm sure you're saying to yourself, "What's the big deal if Buster has to wait two or three hours more before he gets his walk?" I agree with you; that's no big deal. If the truth be known, I can really go for eighteen to twenty hours without a walk. It's not comfortable, but I can do it. It's usually the rain that makes that long a wait necessary though.

The guilt trip that I can put on Andy is incredible if I don't get my walk within a reasonable period of time. I have this little sound that I make, somewhere between a sigh and a whimper. It always gets him. "What's wrong, Buster?" is his first reaction, and he gets that very concerned look on his face which, of course, makes me go into my act even more. I hope I'm not crying "wolf" and when the time comes when something is really wrong, he won't believe me. But as Ms. O'Hara said, "I'll think about that tomorrow." Meanwhile, I've just got to concentrate on new ways to get Andy out of bed on the weekend. Give me a little more time, and I'm sure I'll come up with something.

CHAPTER TWENTY-THREE
"Mirror, Mirror"

There are many firsts in your life, but I don't think there was any first in my life which was more startling than the first time I saw myself in a mirror. Of course, Andy set me up for it, and, I fell for it like a complete sucker.

I couldn't have been more than three months old when Andy and I came back to the apartment from a walk, and Andy picked me up and walked over to a mirror in the front hall that hung above the mail table. I looked at the mirror and to my horror discovered that

Andy had someone else in his arms. This made me quite upset so I began to bark at the little gray thing that was taking my place. And he barked back at me. Andy started to laugh which made me even angrier. Why was Andy siding with this intruder?

And then it dawned on me -I was still in Andy's arms! There wasn't any other animal. Somehow I was seeing me! Let me tell you that's one shock that I won't forget soon. I was so little and so gray. I didn't look like Andy at all. Until then I was sure I was just a smaller version of him, and yet the awful truth was there staring me in the face.

I turned my face away, hoping that when I looked back, I too, would have a face and arms and a torso like Andy, but one quick furtive look made me realize that it was never going to be. He walked on two legs; I walked on four. He was sort of off-white; I was definitely gray. And I had a large mustache.

There was no way we could be mistaken for each other.

I laid my head on Andy's shoulder and put one paw over my face. I didn't want to look into a mirror again for as long as I lived. I think Andy sensed that I was unhappy because he put me down on the floor very gently and sat down next to me.

It's all right, Buster. It's just a reflection of you in the mirror. And you were very safe there in my arms."

I snuggled up next to him, letting him know how much I loved him. But there was no way I could really tell him what a shock it was that we were so different.

Andy got up and went over to his bookcase. He pulled out this rather large book and then sat down next to me again. He opened the book and moved it over where I could see it as well. I couldn't believe what I was seeing! The book was full of pictures of animals that look a lot like me.

Andy said, "You see, Buster, you have lots of beautiful cousins all over the world. These are pictures of just a few of them. You'll meet many more who look like you over the next few years. I know it's a shock to see yourself for the first time, but you see what a handsome lad you are."

I became very interested in seeing the pictures of the other Schnauzers as Andy began reading captions under the pictures. Some of the dogs were champions (of what I didn't know). Others were dogs who belonged to famous people royalty, movie stars, people like that. Andy pointed one dog out and said, "This one belongs to the Duchess of Beaufort, and lives in England in a huge mansion with two thousand acres of park around it. Wouldn't you like to live there?"

I couldn't believe it that he asked me that question, He knows I would never live anywhere except with him. I looked up at him with the best look of disgust I could muster since we Schnauzers are not known for being able to look disgusted. But I think he got the message because he immediately recanted.

"Of course I know you' d rather be here with me."

I licked his hand a couple of times to signify that he had understood me, and we continued to look through the book until we got to the end. I have to confess that I didn't quite make it to the end because after I curled up next to Andy, I drifted off into sleep dreaming of Schnauzers from all over the world who I realized didn't have it half as good as I did. And I pledged to myself never to look into a mirror again.

CHAPTER TWENTY-FOUR
"Home Alone"

I think I was a little over a year old when it happened the first time. Andy got out his suitcases the way he always did when we were going to East Hampton or some other place for the weekend. I got excited as I always did because I love to travel. It's so stimulating, and it definitely sets me apart from those other dogs who try to act so sophisticated but have never been any place other than the street.

Andy was very busy with what he was doing and wasn't

paying any attention to me which is okay. I don't need attention twenty-four hours a day. When he got all his bags packed, I realized he hadn't gotten my carrying case or any of the other accouterments which always accompanied me. Then he finally turned to me and said, "I have to go away on a business trip. I won't be gone long, just three or four days."

Three or four days! A lifetime! We'd never been apart before other than when Andy went to work or went out for business or on a date. This was different. He wouldn't be home at night; he wouldn't be there for me in the morning; life was going to be miserable. How could I make it through?

"But don't worry. I've asked Bill to come over and take care of you every day. He'll feed you and take you for nice long walks."

I was panicked. Bill was a nice enough guy, but he wasn't Andy. He didn't know the secret places on my walks that I liked to take extra sniffs; he didn't know the special places I liked to be rubbed. Life was going to be awful.

With those words, Andy was gone. If schnauzers could cry, I would have so I did the only thing I could to show my grief. I howled, but since nothing happened, I decided I didn't want to get laryngitis, so I stopped. But I hid under the sofa and pretended it was my mourning cave.

When Bill arrived, I came out of my hiding place to greet him at the door. I had been thinking all day that I had to make it clear from the start who the boss was. By that, of course, I mean me.

He gave me a pat on the head and then invited me to have

106

supper. I went into the kitchen while he prepared my food, half from the can and half from the bag of dry food. He put it all in my bowl and set it down. It looked a little skimpy to me so instead of diving right into it the way I always did, I just looked up at him with disgust. I guess I made him feel guilty because he said, "Not enough, huh? Well, you have to remember I'm new at this." With that I got a couple of extra scoops. And Andy would never know!

The real test of whether I could train Bill properly came with the first walk. I knew if I let him get away with anything, I'd never get my way again. Thank goodness it wasn't raining because that would have brought too many complications. What I was going to have to do was complicated enough.

Bill started to turn right outside the front door. Wrong! I liked to go left except when Andy took me to the office, which wasn't very often. I tightened the muscles in my neck, turned my body in the other direction and tugged. At first I thought Bill was going to insist on having his way, but he quickly decided to let me guide him. Step one was victory for me!

There were several spots along the street which were my special spots. They were special to me because they seemed to be special to every dog who ever walked on that block. That meant there were a lot of good smells and sniffs which I was used to having.

Bill apparently came from the school of let's just get it done and over with" which was not going to be alright with me. At my first special spot I found some wonderful new smells which had to be explored fully or else my walk would be ruined. I had just begun to

107

sniff when Bill started to tug at my leash.

"Watch it, mister, "I wanted to say but of course couldn't. Instead, I planted my paws into the ground and stood as stiff as I could. "I will not be moved! " I shouted from my heart. Bill, of course, couldn't hear me. All he could say was, "Buster, that's enough. We've got the whole block to cover."

What did I care what he wanted? This was my walk; I was entitled to it; and I was going to take it my way on my own terms. When he saw I was serious about not budging, Bill relented and said, "Okay, this once, go ahead and take your time. " He was crazy if he thought I was only going to get my way once. He certainly didn't know me very well.

Bill had brought some paper with him the way Andy always did. I wondered if he had a fetish too about my poop. Well, there was only one way to find out. When I came to my favorite manhole cover, I squatted directly over the hole and with great precision pooped right into the hole.

Bill looked confused. He had paper ready in his hand and leaned down to see what had happened. Then he realized I had sent my poop through the hole. "My gosh, Buster, that's incredible. I hope there' s no one down there right now, but I've never seen such aim in my life."

I was truly pleased that he was impressed. In fact, I softened up a little and let him think that he had pulled me away from a couple of smells, but if the truth be known, they weren't very good spots, and I really didn't intend to spend much time there.

I must say that Bill was very punctual and very good about feeding me and taking me out. I was certainly grateful. But that night when I heard footsteps in the hall, I knew it wasn't Bill; Andy had come home! Glory, hallelujah!

I raced to the door, and when Andy walked in and picked me up, I smothered his face in kisses and nuzzles. I was so glad to see him. And he was really glad to see me too. "I missed you, kid," he said.

And even though I couldn't answer him with words, I'm sure the look in my eyes told him everything he needed to know.

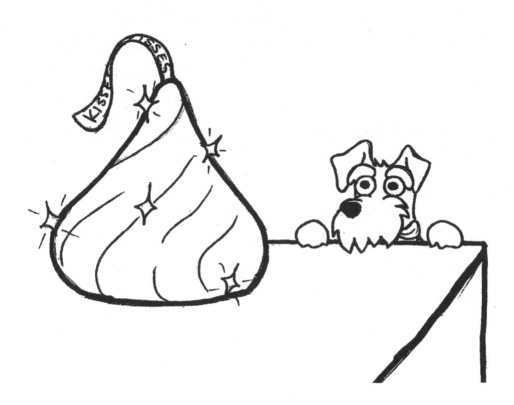

CHAPTER TWENTY-FIVE
"Life is Not a Box of Chocolates"

I have a big confession to make, but don't worry. Andy already knows about it. He had to live through it. I feel as if I almost didn't.

But as you'll see, it wasn't really my fault. Andy's mother Frances sent him a one pound chocolate kiss for Valentine's Day. Now, Andy didn't need any chocolate at all, much less a one pound chunk of it. And he was very good about it; didn't touch a single piece.

I, however, am another story. When Andy left for work, he didn't put the chocolate up high where I couldn't reach it. Instead, he left it on the coffee table in the living room which was a place I often explored for unknown goodies - sometimes some crumbs from last night's pizza - sometimes leftover pieces of dinner the night before. There was never anything substantial, just your basic crumb grazing.

The minute after Andy had left, my nose began to twitch. Something was in the air, and I had to find out what it was. I began to stalk every conceivable spot in the room going in concentric circles from the outside perimeter toward the center. And there it was on the coffee table - a package wrapped in bright green tinfoil just waiting to be explored. There was no doubt about it - there was something wonderful waiting inside.

Using my nose as a bulldozer, I pushed the package onto the floor and quickly tore open the wrapping. A mountain of chocolate was revealed. I took a quick lick to be sure it was as good as it smelled, and it was. Realizing I had hours to work on my treasure, I slowly began to chip away at the sides of the candy. It was manna from heaven - doggie heaven, that is. When I felt I had eaten enough, I went over to lie down in the little patch of sun that shone into the room to take a nap. Then, on waking up, I realized it was time to go back for more.

This went on all day long until the whole candy kiss was a memory. The last couple of times I went back to eat, my stomach wasn't feeling great, but I wasn't going to lose the challenge of finishing that chocolate before Andy came home so I made myself do it. I ate the foil wrapper too, just to be sure.

I finished the last part of the kiss about a half hour before Andy came in the door. He took one look, turned toward me and started screaming. "You bad dog. You know that wasn't for you."

Well, if it wasn't for me, then why did he leave it where I could find it? And come to think of it why did his mother send it in the first place? You see how misunderstood we animals often are. Humans entrap us, and we have to take the blame. Anyway, I did my best impression of a cowering, sad, misunderstood but contrite puppy to try to get Andy off my back. As I was doing this, a feeling began to come over me that something was happening inside my body, and I didn't know what it was. Then, all of a sudden, I erupted and molten chocolate went everywhere - the rug, the coffee table, the sofa. It was awful.

Andy just stood there in total disbelief. "Now look what you've done!" ("mea culpa, mea culpa" is all I could think of). And what about me? What about the way I feel? I mean I was really sick. Think about me, Andy.

I decided the only thing I could do would be to go into the corner, curl up in a ball and disappear. Besides, I was beginning to feel worse and worse so I neither wanted to try to make amends through the usual tail-wagging routine or witness Andy cleaning up the mess which would only make me feel guilty. Retreat was the only solution.

Mutual ignoring took over although I did hear a lot of "ughs" from Andy as he was trying to find ways to restore the furniture and rug to its prior condition. Every "ugh" made me sink deeper into my fetal position and made me resolve not to look up.

113

Andy turned on the news on television, made himself a Diet Pepsi and settled onto the cleaned-up couch. I stayed put. My head was spinning now and my stomach kept turning inside out at the speed of the earth' s rotation. Not good.

My dinner time was fast approaching, I didn't know how I would cope with that. There wasn't a prayer that I could eat even one piece of dry dog food, much less the canned stuff. Even the slightest smell of anything edible would make me sick again. Funnily enough, Andy made no move to get me dinner. Was he punishing me?

This went on until late night walk time when I gingerly arose and allowed my leash to be buckled onto my collar. I won't describe the walk; it was too embarrassing. All I know is that when we got back inside, Andy picked me up and put me on the pillow next to him as he turned out the light to go to sleep. The sadder but wiser dog that I had become groaned a couple of times and then went to sleep.

I awoke the next morning, as I usually did every morning, with my whole backside snuggled against Andy's leg. A new day was here, and even though I wouldn't want food for another twenty-four hours, I knew there was still love in our room.

CHAPTER TWENTY-SIX
"Anywhere He Wanders"

Sometimes Andy would tell me he was going on a "trip". I
didn't know what the word meant. All I knew is that he would be
away from home and away from me for long periods of time. Of
course, since I have no sense of time, I don't really know what a long
time is, but whatever it is, it was with him.

I began to notice a pattern when he said he was going on a
"trip". He would pull this box-like thing out of the closet (I think he
called it a "suitcase" even though Andy almost never wore a suit), he
laid it on the bed and then filled it with clothes. He even took things
from the bathroom like his razor and shaving cream and toothbrush. I

just didn't understand what he was about.

But after a few times of doing this and kissing me good-bye on the cheek, he would be gone, as I said before, for a long time. One of his friends would always come over and stay with me since Andy didn't want me to be alone, but it just wasn't the same. They tried to cheer me up by playing sock or ball or ring-toss with me, but my heart wasn't in it. I wanted Andy at home where I could lick his nose whenever I wanted to.

After witnessing this affair with the " suitcase" several times, I began to get the hang of it. Andy was going on a "trip", and I wasn't. That just didn't seem fair so I had to put my mind to work to make sure I went on that trip as well. I thought maybe I could disguise myself as his sidekick the way I had seen people do on TV, but even though I looked very hard, no disguise costume could be found.

I noticed that he had something he called a passport and something else he called a ticket or sometimes an e-ticket (I didn't know the difference of course) but it seemed to be very necessary for Andy to take his "trip". A plan came to mind which I began to carry out in a very discreet manner.

When Andy went into the bathroom to take his shower, I found the passport and the ticket lying on the bed next to the "suitcase". I reasoned that if I took those and hid them, Andy couldn't leave me. I grabbed both of them and took them under the bed to my special hiding place and quickly rushed out from under the bed looking very innocent. Andy toweled himself off, came into the bedroom and began to get dressed. He hadn't noticed that anything was missing! Not yet, at least.

After finishing dressing, Andy snapped the locks on the "suitcase" shut and looked for his ticket and passport. But of course he couldn't find them. He looked at me, and I could tell he was upset. I raised my face towards his and my big brown eyes have never looked more innocent. If I could blush, I'd do it right now.

Andy kept staring at me and the he finally spoke. "Buster, what have you done with my passport and ticket?" That's pretty direct, I thought.

Since I can't speak English, I didn't answer, but I was beginning to feel very guilty inside. "Do I or don't I" I kept asking myself. Andy asked me again, this time a little sharper.

My face fell and a sheepish look came over it. Andy knew, I'm sure he did. I went under the bed and retrieved the ticket and passport and dropped them at Andy's feet. "What am I in for now" I thought.

But by now you ought to know that Andy is my best friend and I know he wouldn't harm me. But he did surprise me. He laughed and laughed. "Buster, you are too much. Sometimes I just can't believe the things you do."

I wagged my tail, he picked me up and gave me a big hug. "You know I would take you with me if I could, but I just can't. Maybe one of these times we'll go away somewhere together." That did it. I just snuggled into his arms for a last hug before he left.

That was only one battle and I lost it. But I still had a plan.

The next time the suitcase came out I was ready. Andy usually packed before he took his shower to get dressed to leave so I casually

117

observed everything he did and didn't show the least bit of emotion. I suspect that made him curious but he didn't say anything.

He went into the shower; I went into action.

The suitcase was open and his clothes we all laid out inside. The suitcase wasn't too full which was exactly what I had hoped for. I jumped onto the bed and warily began to make a hole for myself through the clothes. When I thought I had enough room, I burrowed in and voila I fit perfectly. Now came the real test. Since I don't have any thumbs (and let me tell you how angry I am at evolution that they were left out of my makeup), I had to use my paws and mouth and somehow I managed to get under the clothes and be hidden.

Andy came back in and got dressed. Then he shut the top of the suitcase and snapped the locks. I suppose that was the point at which he realized I wasn't around so he called out to me "Buster, come in here now."

Of course I couldn't have come there at that point even if I'd wanted to. I was about to take a "trip" even though it was pretty stuffy, uncomfortable and hot in that suitcase. I could hear Andy moving around and calling out to me. He was getting very irritated.

"Buster, enough is enough. You get here this minute." Of course I couldn't. I began to get a little nervous. Did I make the right decision? How long was I going to be trapped inside this suitcase? I decided I had better do something about the situation so I began scratching the inside of the suitcase. Nothing. Where was Andy? Why couldn't he hear me? I was panicking.

All of a sudden I heard the locks being opened and the top of the suitcase was raised. By this time I had gotten on top of most of the clothes, and as Andy looked down into the suitcase he saw me smiling and wagging my tail. My hero!

"Buster, I ought to punish you good for putting a scare like this on me, but as usual I can't resist your face and your tail. All is forgiven." He lifted me gently out of the suitcase and put me on the bed. He leaned down and let me lick his nose.

God' s in his heaven; all's right with the world.

CHAPTER TWENTY-SEVEN
"In the Rotogravure"

It was early April in New York, and when Andy took me for my morning walk, the sun was shining bright and it was warm. All the winter problems seemed to be over. No more snow; no more rock salt on the sidewalks; no more cars splashing muddy slush as they whiz zed by. I was feeling really good and looking forward to lots of warm, sunny days.

It was Sunday (I could tell by the size of the New York Times), which I always loved, because Andy didn't have to go to work and could spend some quality time with me. He read the New York Times, or at least sections that he really liked such as sports, arts & leisure, the week in review, the magazine section, the book review section and travel. He downed two or three cups of coffee, and it looked as if I might have him to myself for the whole day.

The doorbell rang, and there was Betsy standing outside looking like a million dollars and wearing this huge hat with all sorts of things in it. Andy started laughing. I was afraid that Betsy was going to get angry because he was laughing at her, but then she started laughing as well. I couldn't understand what was so funny, but then people can sometimes be so weird.

Andy told Betsy to sit down in the living room, and he'd be ready in a minute. "Oh, no," was all I could think. My plans for the day alone with Andy had been shot. Now he and Betsy were going out, and from the look of what she was wearing, they'd probably be gone all day. I was very sad.

Andy looked ready spiffy when he emerged. He had on his light tan Brooks Brothers poplin suit, Brooks Brothers shirt and tie and Brooks Brothers cordovans which were so shiny I could see my reflection in them. Somehow, though I couldn't muster a lot of enthusiasm at the thought of being left alone on a beautiful Sunday.

I shouldn't have worried. Andy called to me, "Buster, come here and let's put your leash on. We're going to the Easter Parade."

What's Easter? What's a parade? But frankly I didn't care. All I knew was that I wasn't going to be abandoned. I jumped up and ran over to him, my little tail wagging happily. My leash was fastened and

122

off we went.

We walked slowly because Betsy had these high-heeled shoes on. I couldn't believe she could actually walk in them, I know I couldn't have, but she had to be careful. As we walked, she put her arm through Andy's arm which made me a little jealous, but it was so nice just to be going that I let it pass.

By the time we got to Fifth Avenue I could see that the street was mobbed. We stopped in front of St. Patrick's cathedral and walked up a couple of steps to get a better look around. There were ladies in big hats, little hats, crazy hats. Every woman there had a hat on. Maybe that's what Easter means, a time for ladies to wear hats. Or maybe that's "parade". Sometimes I really wish I could talk.

There was such a mob scene when we stepped back down into the street that I began to get claustrophobic. I was also really afraid I'd get stepped on. But Andy held me very tightly next to him, and I was safe. A lot of people, especially women, stooped down to say "hello" to me, and I liked that.

As we walked up the Avenue toward Central Park, I noticed that a number of people had their dogs out for a walk as well. So many of them were wearing hats just like their owners. One French poodle, who was incredibly snobbish, shouldn't have been. If she could have seen herself with a miniature Eiffel Tower on top of her head, I think she would have slunk off into a corner in shame. Thank goodness Andy didn't try to " frill" me up. I hate that kind of thing.

By the time we got to the Plaza Hotel, the crowd had thinned out a little, and Andy gave me more slack to sniff around, which of

123

course, I did gleefully. This was a part of town that was new to me, and the smells were divine! He showed Betsy the fountain that supposedly Scott Fitzgerald and his wife, Zelda, had jumped into one night when they were drunk. The rim was too tall for me to see over so I don't know what it really looks like inside.

Andy asked Betsy if she was hungry since he was. She said "yes", but Andy realized that the Plaza wouldn't let me go in with them for some unknown reason. I thought I was more than presentable and certainly wouldn't do anything to embarrass Andy, but you just can't convince people sometimes when they're set in their ways.

Andy had a great suggestion. "Let's go into the park, and we'll get some take-out and sit on a bench and eat with Buster.

Betsy liked the idea, and I, of course, was ecstatic. Sunday in the park with Andy...and Betsy. What a nice idea!

We walked up through the zoo, and I felt really sorry for all those animals in cages when it was such a beautiful day outside. However, I have to admit that I wasn't too keen about seeing any lions, tigers, or panthers roaming the park while I was in it. I'd just be an appetizer, and the thought of that made me shiver. I knew I didn't need to worry, though. Andy would always protect me.

Betsy held my leash while Andy went up to the stand and bought some food. Then the three of us found a nice, shaded bench to sit on and enjoy lunch. Even I was given a couple of small bites by Andy. I like Easter!

The next night when Andy got home from his office, he had a newspaper with him that I had never seen before. Inside there were two full pages of pictures. Andy showed me the paper, and there was a picture of Andy and Betsy at the Easter Parade. And guess who was sitting at their feet. Me! Oh, how I wished I owned some Porsche sunglasses. I'd make every poodle in New York green with envy.

CHAPTER TWENTY-EIGHT
"Nirvana"

There's one other thing I wanted to tell you about, but I guess I'm a little bit afraid you'll laugh at me. I heard Andy and a friend of his talk about psychiatrists or psychologists or something like that. I didn't know what they were, but when Andy and his friend really got into their discussion, I began to understand.

From the way they were talking, I thought that kind of doctor was only for people, but I heard Andy's friend saying that now these doctors were available for animals too, especially dogs. Even though

127

I know I'm a small gray person, I also know that I'm technically classified as a dog so that makes me included.

Now they had my attention. A psychiatrist for dogs? I wonder what they could do for me? I don't need one because I'm really very well adjusted, have no phobias to speak of and am perfectly behaved. And yet, I have this sneaking suspicion that a doctor like that can help me.

I guess you're wondering what my problem is, right? I'm not ashamed to tell you. I have this recurring dream, and I wonder what it means. Andy kept talking about a man named Freud who would study someone's dreams and analyze the problem, if there was one, from those dreams. I wished I could meet him, but then I found out he was dead.

I've never told anyone about my dream, but I'm going to do it now so that if anyone knows a doctor who can tell me what it means, please do. Don't be afraid, it isn't an awful dream like a nightmare; it's a wonderful dream that I love dreaming. Whenever I do, I always hope it will never stop.

Here goes:

Andy wakes up in the morning and hugs me in bed. I give him lots of kisses and explore his ear, and we don't have to rush to get out of bed or do anything else. Just lie there and enjoy each other's company.

When we do get up, Andy slips on his "morning walk" clothes, and we do our usual thing around the block. But Andy is in no hurry, and I get every sniff I could possibly want without any suggestion that we have to hurry.

We get back to the apartment and have breakfast. Andy shaves and showers and packs a suitcase. At first I'm afraid that I'll be left behind, but he packs some things for me so I know I'll be traveling with him. Mirabile dictu!

This time, there' s a difference. We don't go to the train station but to a place that rents cars, and Andy rents one. He packs the car, I settle down in my curl position on the other front seat, and off we go to somewhere. I find I really like riding in a car. It's not like the taxis that swerve in and out of traffic and scare me half to death. And Andy doesn't make sudden stops that almost throw you onto the floor. Also, he doesn't yell obscenities to another driver for doing something that a taxi driver doesn't like. It's a lot more civilized to drive with Andy in a rented car.

We drive for what seems like hours and then stop for food. Of course, I get a little walk as well which is nice because driving does make me need to walk more often than lying on the rug at home. I also get a nice cool drink of water because Andy never forgets that his little friend has needs, too.

We drive until it begins to get dark, and Andy pulls off the road and finds a motel. It's a nice one because they have room service, and if there' s one thing both Andy and I have in common, it's a love for room service. Andy just goes down this menu and decides to have one of those and one of those; and he orders some special treat for me. It's not a full dinner, but it's always a wonderful surprise. I still get my usual dinner, but I get to eat it off motel china which always makes it taste better. I pretend it's some exotic food that I've never had before. I heard Andy once talk about this really expensive food called "caviar" so I pretend that's what my dinner is. It works for me.

The next day we drive and drive, but this time when we stop, it isn't at a motel. We're in front of this wonderful house with lots of trees and flowers all around it, and it's absolutely private. You can't see another house or another human being anywhere. It's on a hill and in the distance you can see the ocean with sunlight dancing off the top of little whitecaps which the wind has created in the water. I had to catch my breath.

The house isn't big; just one bedroom and bath, but it has a beautiful kitchen and a huge living room with a wood-burning fireplace. As if by magic, a beautiful fire is burning when we walk in. In front of the fireplace is a thick rug just aching to be curled up on, and I couldn't wait to do it. I could see it now: Andy is reading his book (he reads a lot), and I'm daydreaming in front of the fire.

I didn't get a chance to explore the property very much when we got there because I wanted to see the house, and we were both tired from the trip. But bright and early Andy takes me outside without a leash (hallelujah!), and I'm free to run to my heart's content. Somehow Andy lets me go wherever I want to go because he knows that nothing will happen to me. For the first time in my life I'm truly free! And it feels great.

I smell the flowers which are all around, and I don't lift my leg on them, only on the weeds. I've also discovered that digging in the dirt is really my thing so I go at it with a vengeance.

Then I notice the most amazing thing: all the beautiful trees don't have leaves. They're growing dog biscuits. And the bushes are filled with dog biscuits. Some of them are so low that I can reach up and take one without straining at all. Others I have to stand on my hind legs to get. And the rest Andy plucks and gives to me.

You'd think I would eat so many biscuits from all this that I'd get so fat I would pop. But a miracle occurs. I can eat as many as I like, and I never get full nor even gain weight. I can't explain it, but you can bet I take advantage of it. Also, I remember hearing someone say that if you eat too much of a good thing, you'll then lose your taste for it and never want it again. Well, I can tell you it never happens. I pop biscuits like a starlet pops bon-bons, and I love it!

Andy shows me a door to the outside with a small door carved out of the bottom. All I have to do is put my nose against it, and it will open and let me go outside. Any time I want to! Andy thinks of everything.

There's always music playing and birds singing. It's as if we were cut off from the world. I have a special patch of shady grass I sleep on when I feel like being bucolic and a wonderful rug in front of the fire when I want to be inside. Andy is very happy and pays a lot of attention to me whenever I want him to. We live a very quiet and peaceful life, and Andy looks at me and says, "What do you think, Buster, shall we stay here always?"

It's always at the point when I'm just about to answer that I wake up and realize where I am. Then I get just a little sad. Maybe that's why a good psychiatrist can tell me what my dream means.

131

But no matter what it means, Andy is still my best friend in the whole world, and I know that new adventures are just around the corner.

CHAPTER TWENTY-NINE
"Howl"

Dogs howl and/or bark at sirens. I am a dog. Ergo, I howl and/or bark at sirens. That's pure logic, but it's true. The question is "Is that all I howl at?" The answer to that is "no" because there are any number of things that hurt my sensitive ears and cause me to howl or bark.

When I was younger, I almost never howled at anything. A police car could go screaming past me on the street, and I would pay no attention. A fire truck or a procession of fire trucks could go roaring past and I would continue to sniff the grass as unconcerned as I could be. Then one day everything changed.

I can't explain what happened. Maybe it was my growing older or maybe it was just that I began to hear more things than I had in the past. I can't be exact about this but one day as an ambulance came screeching through the street, I stopped, turned toward the noise and lifted by head in the air and out came this howl as if I had been stabbed by a dull knife. You wouldn't believe the look on Andy's face when I did that.

"Buster, what are you doing?"

That was a dumb question. I was doing what every other dog was doing - howling at an ambulance.

"You've never done that before."

Again, does he think I don't know that? The ambulance moved on and as Andy stroked my head to get me to calm down, I began to howl softer until it was all gone. But I had definitely found my howl zone, and I was determined to keep it. Frankly, I rather liked letting off a little steam that way. I felt a little like king-of-the-hill when it was all over.

That night while Andy and I were watching television, we heard a dog bark from the screen. I wasn't sure where it really came from but I let that dog know that he couldn't bark at me in my house without a response so I made a couple of sharp replies. This again startled Andy.

"Barking at the television now? First the siren and now the TV? This is a new chapter in your life."

I decided that now that I had established that I could counter anything that happened on TV through my own voice, TV was sometimes a challenge but basically a good thing.

Except that I cannot stand to hear bells on the TV - no telephones, no churches and especially no school bells so I put my head down into the burrows of the couch and try to cover my ears with my paws. But I still bark at some of the dogs on the TV, especially if they bark at me first. However, so far none of them have come out of the TV to attack me so I guess they're all afraid of my bark.

I have found that my howling at sirens seems to be contagious. A few months ago when I was out for a walk with Andy, a fire truck came along making its usual ear-splitting noise, I began to howl, and to my surprise Andy began to howl with me. He's not as good at it as I am, but he's trying. He doesn't do it every time, but when he does it, it would make me laugh if I could laugh, but since I can't, I smile in my head where no one can see it. But I know it's there.

As you can tell, I have now come to grips with my howling. I will howl at every fire truck, every police car and every ambulance.

But I refuse to bay at the moon. I have my standards.

CHAPTER THIRTY
"Higher Than High"

As I pointed out earlier, one of my pet (please pardon the pun) peeves with Andy is that he never lets me eat the delicious and interesting things I find on the sidewalks of New York. [Sometimes there's a bit of pizza (pepperoni is my favorite); sometimes there's a piece of a bagel which with luck may have a little cream cheese or a sliver of lox on it.]

I could go on and on about the finds I have made and will continue to make. Andy has said something about bad people might try to poison me by leaving a tempting piece of meat on the sidewalk. I'm not sure what poison is, but Andy says it would be very bad for me and make me die.

So to make a short story even shorter, Andy is extremely strict and if I find a morsel that seems interesting and try to put it my mouth or actually get it into my mouth, Andy will immediately reach in and try to make me give it up. That makes me very angry because "finders, keepers" and I found it. Sometimes he gets it and sometimes he doesn't if I'm really quick and it's easy to swallow whole.

Andy keeps asking me "Don't you get enough food at home when I feed you? That stuff's expensive and you should just eat that and you don't need anything more."

Since I can't talk, I just look at him, but if I could talk I would Say, "You don't understand. Half the fun is finding things you're never allowed to eat at home and popping them into your mouth on the street. We schnauzers are hunters and this is the closest thing we'll ever get to it in New York City. "

I suspect he would understand me or agree with me if I could tell him that so I guess it's just as well that we continue our standoff. Because I am not going to stop hunting, and he's never going to stop trying to get me to stop.

I have to tell you about one of my experiences, however, when I was foraging on the street during one of my walks with Andy. We weren't going fast since I was deliberately taking my time and looking feverishly for something to munch on. I happened to spot something brown a short distance ahead, and I realized I had to distract Andy somehow so he wouldn't see me slipping it into my mouth. I don't know why, but for some reason it looked especially delicious.

138

Just as I got to the morsel, I turned around toward Andy and saw he was talking with a friend across the street, and I began to bark and look behind him. This diverted his attention just enough for me to grab the brown morsel, savor it very briefly and scarf it down without Andy seeing me. To tell you the truth it was sweet and very good, sort of like a cookie or piece of cake.

When we got back upstairs, I felt sleepy so I went to my favorite spot on the couch, curled up and went to sleep. I guess I slept pretty well because when Andy called me to come get my supper, I couldn't believe it was time to eat. But I was really hungry as he plated my dish with my usual dog food and a bright orange carrot to top it off. I ate it all with relish.

Not long after supper I got to go over to Andy's chair where he was sitting, and my legs began to wobble a bit, and my head was spinning. I had never felt like this before and I wasn't sure how to react. Andy looked down at me and said, "Buster, what's the matter?" I just stared.

Andy leaned down to pick me up and as his hand came toward me, I quickly backed away from him. I don't know why, but I was suddenly afraid of him and his hand. I saw this hurt and quizzical look on Andy's face.

"Buster, it's me, Andy, what's the matter?"

I didn't know what was wrong; I only knew that I couldn't stand up straight, couldn't walk straight and felt very funny. And then all of a sudden I started racing around the apartment like a crazy dog. This got Andy even more worried. He managed to catch me and scoop

139

me up at which I began to squirm and try to get out of his grasp, something I had never done before.

Andy put me down and said, "Buster, we're going to the vet. Something is really wrong." He put on his coat and tied my collar and leash on my neck and we raced out of the front door to a taxi.

When we got to our usual vet, we found they had closed for the night so we jumped into a taxi and headed in another direction. The new vet was open and when they asked what was wrong, Andy told the receptionist " I think my dog has had a stroke. I really need to have someone see him now."

Very shortly a lovely young woman vet came out and took me from Andy into the back of the clinic and began to look into my eyes, feel my pulse, check my heart, I don't remember what else. And then she called Andy to come back. She told him, "I see no signs of a stroke at all. It could be some other kind of brain thing but I can't see any signs of such. I'm really baffled, but if he were my dog, I would take him to an animal hospital where they have more to work with."

Andy thanked her and looked at me. "Come on, Buster, we have one more stop to make. We've got to find out what caused this."

I was still pretty groggy so don't take every word I'm dictating as actual fact. It's just the best I can do from the condition I was in. And if you want to know the truth, my spirits were good and I was happy without really knowing why.

We drove to an animal hospital which wasn't too far away and again Andy told the receptionist that I had probably had a stroke and we needed to see a doctor right away. In a minute a lovely Chinese doctor came out to reception and said, "Hello, I'm Dr. Han. What can I do for you?"

Andy explained again what had happened and how I had been acting, and again the doctor took me into the back while Andy waited in reception. I had all the same thing done to me again, and again Andy was called back.

Dr. Han said, "We've checked all of Buster's vitals. We don't find any evidence of a stroke, and we're pretty positive he didn't have one. We do now believe we know what happened."

"Is it serious?" Andy seemed very worried.

"No, it will pass in a couple of days, maybe sooner."

"What do I need to do?" Andy still had a worried tone.

"Just make sure he gets plenty of rest and water and food. He'll be alright, I assure you." Dr. Han smiled brightly.

"You don't have any medicine for me to give him or anything like that?"

"No, just do as I said. Buster is having a high right now. He's eaten some marijuana, probably in a brownie, while you were walking him earlier. He's just in a marijuana fog and will come out of it."

Andy looked down at me, trying to look stern, but I could tell he was trying to keep from laughing. "If you hadn't made me so anxious and upset, Buster, I wouldn't be able to stop laughing."

All things considered, it wasn't a bad experience, but I think for everyone's sake from here on in, anything brown that looks like a cookie is off limits.

CHAPTER THIRTY-ONE
"On Top of the World"

I guess I led a pretty sheltered life in our apartment even though I did get to Central Park and the Hamptons and a few other wonderful places. But I never got to see what New York City really looked like up on top of all those tall buildings I would see whenever Andy and I went for a walk together.

The buildings were so big and tall that many times there wasn't any sunlight at all to walk in and that made me sad because the sun always made me feel warm and somehow loved. That may sound crazy but the warmth of the sun was a lot like the warmth of lying next to my mother when I was first born. I felt safe there. It's the same way I feel now when I curl up next to Andy. I am untouchable by anything bad.

Andy came home one night and said to me, "Buster, you've got a treat in store tonight. We're having drinks with Elise Maynard at her penthouse."

I know I was supposed to be overjoyed, but who was this Elise person and what is a penthouse. I wondered if it was something like a doghouse only bigger so that a human could live in it.

I guess Andy saw the quizzical look on my face and said, "Of course you don't know who Elise is, but she was a huge star on Broadway many years ago. And she lives in this penthouse with a huge wrap-around terrace with a view of all of New York."

I have to admit I didn't understand everything he was saying and I did wonder how a star could have escaped from the sky to live on a big terrace, but I realized once I got there, maybe everything would become clear.

We got a cab and drove uptown to Eighty-Sixth Street (at least that's what Andy told the driver) and went into a building I'd never been in before. It was nice and had a lobby much bigger than the one in our building. There was a man all dressed up in a uniform with a lot of gold ropes hanging off his shoulder and a cap with those same gold ropes on them. I thought maybe he was a general like the pictures I'd seen in some of Andy's magazines. He ushered us into a beautiful elevator and closed the door. We zoomed upward for what seemed like forever and then he opened the gate and we got out into a nice foyer with two doors. The general said to us "It's the apartment on the left."

Andy knocked and the door was answered by a small lady in a black dress with a white apron and a little white cap on her head. She had a funny accent for which I think Andy asked her if it was French, and she said "wee" which I guess meant "yes". Whatever!

The small lady led us into this huge room with lots of windows running down one side and a door in the middle leading to what looked like a yard. The room had a very long piano, maybe seven feet, with a lot of framed photographs on top of a beautiful shawl which covered a big part of the piano. And there in a huge over-stuffed easy chair sat this incredible lady.

I couldn't tell how old she was except that I knew she was a lot older than Andy. I thought maybe she was his mother whom I had never met. Andy ran to her and threw his arms around her and said "Elise, I am so happy you called and asked us up. And that goes for Buster too."

She looked me over as if I were a prized painting or a piece of Kobe beef and said "Buster. Is that the name you gave him?" She didn't say it in a way that made me think she approved of my name. Well, as you know, neither did I so I loved her immediately. I went up close to her so she could scratch my ear which she willingly did.

"Yes, his name is Buster. I just didn't want to give him some sissy name."

"Why don't we take Buster out on the terrace and let him sniff some air and see the sights." I wagged my tail ferociously to indicate

145

my approval.

Andy looked at me and saw my tail. "I think he's all for it."

The terrace was huge. I could run as hard as I wanted to and then turn around and run the other way. It was a dream come true. When I had tired myself out a bit, Andy picked me up and a looked out on an unbelievable sight. There were lights everywhere. I was looking down on a lot of those buildings I had always looked up at and I couldn't believe what I saw.

Once when we were in the Hamptons, Andy was playing with me in the yard on a beautiful summer night and rolled me over on my back. When I looked up I saw this black sky that twinkled with thousands of lights and it was beautiful. I felt that's what I was doing all over again except this time it was from a different angle.

Andy put me down and then showed me how to stand on my hind legs and put my paws on the top of the wall of the terrace. Balanced like this I could really take in all the lights from one side to the other. It was like being on Fifth Avenue at Christmas time except a thousand times more lights than even that. I just stood there, mesmerized.

Elise said, "I think Buster is impressed."

Andy replied, "I know he is; I've never seen him so quiet." I gave a small bark just to let Andy know I was going to get my word in as well. Then we went back inside.

Elise said. " I want to know how you're doing."

"I'm doing fine. I just hadn't seen you in a good while which is what makes me glad that you called me to get together again. But not to play bridge. You' re too good for me." I wondered if this was true because I had watched Andy play bridge with friends and many of them said how good he was.

"Oh, I get enough bridge playing in at the Cavendish Club so we can dispense with that. Besides you know what stakes I always play for."

"Yes, a dollar a point. I play for 1/10th of a cent per point."

"Elise pooh-poohed, "That's not gambling. That's pretending."

"And that's why we won't ever be able to play." I saw Andy decide he needed to change the subject because it might be getting touchy. "When are going to do a Broadway musical again."

"I believe there's a one word answer for that -never!"

"Please don't say that. But you don't really mean it, do you?"

"I mean it. They aren't writing parts for me the way they used to."

"Sure they are. Broadway needs you."

Elise picked up a little silver bell and rang it. Then she called out "Nanette!" She turned to Andy and said, "That's not her real name but I loved the musical and she doesn't mind. Anyway, it sounds French so what the hell."

Nanette came in. "Wee, wee". That reminded me it was time for my walk.

"Bring us a large shaker of martinis and some caviar and blinis with all the trimmings." Elise turned to Andy. "It's time for some serious drinking."

147

No need to go into more explanation. By some miracle we got home before Andy had completely passed out. Luckily I had sneaked out onto the terrace while he and Elise were lifting their glasses high and had my nightly walk under the stars on a beautiful penthouse terrace.

CHAPTER THIRTY-TWO
"Pay Attention"

I know I'm probably going to sound like a diva, but I just want you to know that I'm not one. But I do have certain rules of behavior that I like to see followed, and if they aren't, then I have to do something about it.

Rule number one is that I cannot stand to be ignored. Can you? I didn't think so. But since I don't speak English, I have to resort to other things in order to make it clear that I need attention and I need it when I want it, where I want it and only if I want it. That isn't so hard for anyone to understand and do now, is it?

As for the morning, I have already given up being able to go for a walk as our first activity. That goes to the making of the coffee which seems to be a ritual that can never be broken. I personally don't care for coffee so I don't know what the fuss is, but Andy will not change his ways at all. I have tried a couple of times to let him know I really needed to go outside before coffee, but he just ignored me because I think he knew I was faking. I don't know how he reads my mind so well.

Luckily, coffee doesn't take that long to make, and we do leave before it has finished brewing so it's really not too bad.

And the morning walk is always brisk and nice. In fact, it gets me all invigorated for the day's activities, including stretching, scratching, yawning, sleeping, eating and generally doing a few dog things. Since I don't do windows, there's no housework for me.

Andy has two papers delivered to our front door every day. Sometimes I hear whoever brings it and I give a few barks to let them know I don't want them to come in. But other times the papers just seem to appear miraculously. If so, he picks them up and takes them to the kitchen while he pours a big cup of coffee. Then he puts some food down for me which I generally eat pretty quickly.

Now comes the part which really annoys me. Andy takes the papers and goes to the couch, sits down, turns on the reading lamp and then ignores me. Me! His constant companion who is always there for him no matter what is being totally ignored.

Well I have devised a few things that work even though I have to confess that Andy doesn't seem to like any of them a whole lot. My first foray into not being ignored is that I will jump up on the couch, go over to Andy and put my head under the paper he's reading and quickly jerk my head up which stops Andy's reading in its tracks. Sometimes he tries to ignore it when I do that, but by the third time, he starts to get annoyed and says "Buster, cut it out. I'm reading the paper." As if I didn't know. If I do it again, he usually picks me up and puts me on the floor.

I have a solution for that too, though. I jump back onto the couch and go over to Andy, put my paws on his shoulder and begin to lick his face very gently. That usually gets a nice remark or too from Andy so I go right on doing it until he says "OK, that's enough. Now let me read the papers." I'm supposed to go lie down at the other end of the couch when he says this so I do, but I'm just plotting what to do next.

Once Andy is through with a section of the paper, he usually tosses it to the end of the couch. Well, after several sections pile up, there's a nice accumulation of paper. And what's a pile of paper for if not for a doggie to play in it.

At first I just rattle some of the pages with my paws, but if that doesn't get a rise out of Andy, then I'll start to dig into the pile and the papers begin to scatter. This usually gets a dirty look which will eventually turn into a "Buster, lie down and stop playing with the papers" said sharply even though I know there's a lot of love in it.

By this time Andy is totally distracted from his papers, and if you want to know the truth, I think he's read about all he wants to read for the day because he takes the clicker and turns the TV on to watch

"The Today Show". Often he's finished his first cup of coffee so he tells me to stay on the couch, and he goes and gets a refill cup. Then he comes back and settles into his TV watching.

This is when I know it's my time to go over to him and curl up next to him, which I do. He puts his hand on my back and scratches it which means he knows I'm there and I know I've won his attention.

Victory is sweet.

CHAPTER THIRTY-THREE
"Surprise!"

It was just the end of another day as it always was, and Andy was at the front door fumbling with his keys while I sat eagerly inside the door wagging my tail and waiting for him to open the door. It was also a Friday which was special because it meant I had Andy for two whole days.

When he came in, he picked me up which was unusual and hugged me to him. "Have I got a surprise for you!"

I looked at his hands to see what delicious morsel of food he had brought for me, but there was nothing there. If not a special treat, what could the surprise be?

Just at that moment Paula and Betsy came in with Brick right behind them. Paula spoke first. "This isn't true, is it? Tell me it isn't."

"It's true," replied Andy.

What was going on? They all knew something that I didn't, and it must be bad from the way they were reacting. Why did Andy make me think the surprise was a good one? I was beginning to worry now.

"Not la-la land?" It was Betsy.

"La-la land it is. At least for a while." Andy didn't look unhappy at all. But what was la-la land?

Tim looked almost tearful. "Why do you want to take that job in California? It's so far away. And you're a confirmed New Yorker. You'll wither on the vine and die out there."

So la-la land was in California. At least we were getting somewhere.

"Thanks for your kind words of support," Andy said sarcastically. "It's only five or six hours away by airplane. They have faxes and Federal Express and all that good stuff. Besides, I'll probably be back and forth a lot."

Paula chimed in, "That's not the point. You don't belong in L. A. You belong here. Is the job offer that much better?"

"I'm afraid so. It's a great opportunity."

This sounded serious to me. Leave New York? Get on an airplane? Andy hadn't even consulted me. New York was my home; I don't count those few weeks in Kansas as anything but a

154

concentration camp. All my smells were here. My favorite trees and manhole covers. All of them were in New York. Wasn't California a big desert? Just the thought of getting all that sand between my toes make me shudder. I was very sad.

When everyone had gone, Andy sat down on the sofa and invited me up. I decided he'd have to beg me since he had betrayed me like this. He didn't beg; he scooped me up and laid me across his leg. I knew we were about to have a serious talk because this was Andy's "serious" mode.

"Buster, we're going to L.A. That's Los Angeles, California, U.S.A. It's very beautiful out there. Lots of sunshine and trees and warm weather. We're going to have our own house; I'm already talking to some real estate agents about it. We want a big backyard with a pool and Jacuzzi. The streets are lined with trees full of birds and squirrels and other things. You're going to love it."

There were an awful lot of words that I didn't understand, like "squirrels" and "pool" and "Jacuzzi", but I realized I'd find out what they were soon enough. I thought it best just to lick his hand and play dumb.

Andy took my licks as a sign of acceptance. What else could I do but accept? I didn't want to be with anyone but him so as the Bible says, "Whither thou goest, I goest too" or something like that.

The next morning Andy was up early which meant that I was up early as well. "Okay, Buster, pack your bags. We're shipping things out on Monday."

Pack my bags? Was he kidding? He knew I didn't know how

155

to pack. That was his job, and I wasn't going to even grace his suggestion with a nod or a lick. He decided to go to California; he'll pack the bags.

On our walk, I saw the snobby little poodle, and as I passed her I said, "We're moving to California; I hope you freeze your tight little tush next winter." Then I tossed my head and pranced on down the street. She was speechless which made me very happy. Always leave 'em with their mouths hanging open.

CHAPTER THIRTY-FOUR
"It's My Party"

I don't understand people again. Why is a sorrowful event the cause for a party. Here we are, Andy and I, going away from New York forever, and what do all his friends want to do? Have a party! I wondered whether I could really get into the party mood as the walls of my house are being brought down as I stand in the ruins.

It didn't make it any easier that morning when I ran into Mitzi, the dachshund I sometimes see on my walks. She had been to Los Angeles once, and she told me it's really hot there most of the time and that I was going to be very sorry I had a fur coat on. That's really

157

stupid of her; how am I supposed to get rid of it? But I supposed that Andy would keep me groomed more in Los Angeles so I wouldn't feel the heat too much.

By the time the party came around, our house was nothing but a pile of boxes, except, of course, there was still furniture. We didn't have one nice thing to serve any food or drink in, but it was okay to use paper plates, plastic glasses and cutlery. Everyone knew the score.

I guess there must have been thirty or forty people weaving in and out among the boxes, and they all seemed to be having a good time. Were they really that happy to see us go? I couldn't believe they were. There was a lot of hugging of Andy by everyone and lots of "we're gonna miss you" and "think about us always". There were also the threats of "you never know when we're gonna show up on your front doorstep and stay for two weeks". Andy took them all in stride and always seemed to know exactly the right answer to use.

For most of the party, all I tried to do was avoid being trampled to death. I managed to find a wonderful cave made by several boxes which weren't pushed up together, and I used that as my base for foraging for party food or begging for a little if the coast was clear.

I heard Andy say he had bought a used car from a friend of his from Long Island and that we were going to drive to Los Angeles. Now that's what I call an adventure in the making, and I must say it perked my spirits up considerably. If there was one thing I liked to do, it was to travel. And all the way across the country was sure traveling.

The party lasted pretty late because when Andy finally took me for my late-night walk, there weren't many people around, and I didn't see one dog I could say good-bye to. That seems a little unfair since Andy said good-bye to all of his friends. But that's the life of a dog.

When Andy and I got in bed, Andy said to me just before he went to sleep, "Get a good night's rest. Tomorrow the movers come, and we leave for California."

True to Andy's word, at seven in the morning the movers were there to take the furniture and all the big boxes. It took them hours to empty the apartment of everything except the things we were taking with us. By the time they had gone I looked around at what it must have been like in Berlin after the war. The reality of all this truly sank in at that moment. I wished I could cry real tears, but that's a gift that wasn't given to me for some reason.

Andy appeared sad, too. He just walked around the apartment checking the closets and the cupboard and anything else he could think of. I don't know if he really thought he hadn't packed something or if he was just using that as an excuse not to deal with really moving away.

Then the time came for us to pack the car and close and lock the front door for the last time. I think both Andy and I had lumps in our throats (yes, at least I can do that) as we went down the elevator for the last time.

Brick had the car waiting for us at the front door. They hugged good-bye, and Brick picked me up and hugged me, too. I liked that.

And then I settled into a big, fluffy pillow strapped into the back seat, and we rode off into the sunset even though it was only

159

eleven-thirty in the morning but we were heading west. Andy started happily singing 'Hooray for Hollywood'. Suddenly I knew everything was going to be great. A wonderful new adventure lay ahead.

I was no longer a New York dog.

THE END

ABOUT THE AUTHOR

CHANDLER WARREN (Author)

Chandler Warren's many stage and lyric writing credits include the book and lyrics for the award-winning musical ADAM AND EVE AND STEVE. It was named best musical at the Hollywood Fringe Festival, followed by a sell-out production at the Edinburgh Theatre Festival. This led to a London production at the Kings Head Theatre, and soon it will be filmed in Hollywood for a digital release. He is currently writing DIARY OF A HOLLYWOOD DOG, and a personal memoir KEEP THE EGGS MOVING, tracing his upbringing in the deep south, through his life as a writer, lyricist, script doctor, producer, and as an entertainment attorney in New York City. He also wrote over forty episodes of the soap opera "Texas" for NBC.

CONTRIBUTORS

STEVEN NASH (Editor/Publisher)

Steven Nash heads Arts and Letters Entertainment, representing actors, writers, producers, and directors. Other pursuits include, producing, directing, and he has been a creative consultant on a wide range of projects. He began his career in New York City as a director and acting coach, where he studied under Stella Adler. Now located in Los Angeles, he is the former president of the Talent Managers Association.

ALASTAIR BAYARDO (Illustrator)

Alastair Bayardo is a self-taught artist who has built a reputation for his work in a wide array of mediums. He is also known as: "BAD ARTIST" on social media. He has several large acrylic pieces that are on display in such cities as Los Angeles and Miami. Alastair is an equally popular mural artist, with commercial installations, and street art including entire buildings and the sides of high rises. He has created many digital illustrations and logos for branding and film marketing. You may also have seen Alastair as an actor on many network tv shows and films. You can find his artwork at www.celebritiesoncanvas.com

BRETT DAVIDSON (Book Designer)

Brett Davidson has created posters, artwork, branding, and other conceptual design in a range of industries and applications. His work includes the commemorative 77th Academy Awards Oscar poster, the Hollywood Walk of Fame logo, graphic design for Sony Pictures, and book design for a large range of fiction and nonfiction titles.

Want to know what really happens behind the cameras?

Premiering soon!